TRAGIC GROUND

Books *by* ERSKINE CALDWELL

Novels:

TOBACCO ROAD
GOD'S LITTLE ACRE
JOURNEYMAN
TROUBLE IN JULY
ALL NIGHT LONG
GEORGIA BOY
TRAGIC GROUND

Volumes of Short Stories:

AMERICAN EARTH
WE ARE THE LIVING
KNEEL TO THE RISING SUN
SOUTHWAYS
JACKPOT
STORIES BY ERSKINE CALDWELL
(edited, with introduction, by Henry Seidel Canby)

Social Studies:

SOME AMERICAN PEOPLE
YOU HAVE SEEN THEIR FACES
(with Margaret Bourke-White)

Travel:

NORTH OF THE DANUBE
(with Margaret Bourke-White)
SAY! IS THIS THE U.S.A.
(with Margaret Bourke-White)

War Correspondence:

ALL-OUT ON THE ROAD TO SMOLENSK
MOSCOW UNDER FIRE
RUSSIA AT WAR
(with Margaret Bourke-White)

Tragic

Ground

BY ERSKINE CALDWELL

New York

DUELL, SLOAN AND PEARCE

A WARTIME BOOK

THIS COMPLETE EDITION IS PRODUCED
IN FULL COMPLIANCE WITH THE GOVERN-
MENT'S REGULATIONS FOR CONSERVING
PAPER AND OTHER ESSENTIAL MATERIALS

PRINTED IN THE UNITED STATES OF AMERICA
AMERICAN BOOK—STRATFORD PRESS, INC., NEW YORK

FOR
JUNE

Tragic
Ground

CHAPTER ONE

SPENCE DOUTHIT HAD SPENT THE WHOLE day trying to buy a bottle of Maud's favorite stomach tonic on credit somewhere. It was late in the hot August afternoon when he got back to Poor Boy and, as he was walking wearily along the ship canal within sight of the weather-grayed bungalow with the rusty tin roof, he was surprised to hear music coming from his house.

He had gone to every drug store, market, and Chinese grocery he could find in the South Side but, even though most of the merchants had a plentiful supply of the tonic, when they found out that he had no money in his pocket, each one of them shook his head firmly and put the bottle back on the shelf. When he finally gave up and started home, he was tired and discouraged. There had been a time when he had never bothered to go out of his way to trade with a Chinaman, and now the Chinamen would not go out of their way to trade with him.

Stopping and turning his head to one side like a dog

3

pricking up his ears at a familiar sound, Spence listened hopefully to the throbbing dance tune. It was the kind of music that Libby liked, and which, at any time of the day or night, she could always find on the radio.

When he was convinced that the sounds were not coming from any of the other nearby houses, he took his hands out of his pockets, the uncertain smile on his face stretching into a broad grin, and hurried home.

"That's her, all right!" he said aloud to himself. "That's Libby!"

Taking the short-cut across Chet Mitchell's front yard for the first time since they had had their most recent fight, Spence ran up the steps two at a time and flung open the screendoor. As he stepped inside, panting and out of breath, his wife rose up expectantly from her cot, supporting herself on her elbows, and watched him as he crossed the room. When he got to the corner where she lay, Maud was looking at him beseechingly. Her brown eyes were unusually large and round, and her skin was flushed and feverish. The flimsy rayon nightgown, the only piece of clothing she had worn that summer, and which had cost ninety-eight cents when it was a much brighter pink, slipped down over her breasts. The shoulder straps had broken so many times that she had stopped trying to keep them mended.

"Libby's home, ain't she?" Spence said excitedly, turning and looking around the room. "I could hear the radio going when I was 'way down the street by the canal. I just knew it was Libby! It's her kind of music!" He

4

moved away from the cot as if to go in search of her. "Where's she at, Maud?"

Maud caught his arm in a desperate grip before he could get away. Her sharp fingernails cut into his flesh painfully, and when he tried to pull his arm free, she held on to him more tightly than ever. While she was drawing him to the cot, Spence glanced behind him at the closed door to the other bedroom, wondering why Libby had shut it on such a hot day. Usually when the elder of his two daughters came to the house for a visit, which she generally did once a week, she took off her clothes, like Chet Mitchell's wife, Myrt, and slept through the hot part of the day. Then when it was cool enough to dress, she would get up and listen to the radio for several hours. This was the first time she had closed the door and stayed in the room so late in the afternoon.

Maud gave his arm a sharp jerk.

"Did you get Dr. Munday's for me, Spence?" she asked weakly, her thin voice all but lost in the din of music that blared from the radio.

Spence fidgeted nervously. He wanted to find Libby right away but, after noticing the despairing look on Maud's face, he realized he would have to wait until he had explained why he had failed to bring back a bottle of tonic. He sat down on the edge of the cot, chewing the tip of his tongue. After a while he felt the tight grip on his arm relax. Turning his head, he watched Maud while she ran her fingers absent-mindedly over her chest in search of the nightgown, wondering why she bothered to wear the gown at all, because the shoulder straps were

5

useless and the gown was always slipping off and becoming lost. The last time she had lost it, they had spent the better part of two days looking for it before he finally found it under the kitchen stove.

"You went and came back without it," she said accusingly. "You didn't get Dr. Munday's for me."

"Don't get all feathered-out before I can explain what a hard time I had, Maud," he said quickly.

She dropped backward on the cot, her head falling heavily to the pillow. She lay there breathing fitfully while he wondered what he could tell her. He felt sorry for her, because he knew how disappointed she was, but he could think of nothing to say that would take the place of tonic. He laid his hand on her shoulder and patted her tenderly. Maud opened her eyes, surprised by the unexpected attention.

"It seems like I went to every last store I could find on the whole South Side," he told her earnestly, trying to make the tone of his voice sound apologetic and hoping the fact that he had made an effort to get a bottle would give her some comfort. "Dogbite it, I couldn't find nobody, not even a Chinaman, to trust me for a teeninecy little thing like that. It sure does get discouraging when even the Chinamen won't give me a little credit."

She picked up his hand and threw it away from her as though she expected to hit the wall on the other side of the room with it.

"I ought to have better sense by this time to think you'd find a way to get me a little thing that I need as

6

bad as I do the tonic," she said resignedly, her breath completely exhausted by the time she had finished.

Spence picked at the loose threads on the quilt while she closed her eyes helplessly.

"Maud, whether you know it or not, these people down here in this part of the world just aint like the folks back home," he said, leaning towards her. "Of course, nobody in his right mind would expect the Mexicans and Chinamen to be a bit different than they are, because being foreigners they don't know better, but even the niggers down here are persnickity, and the whites aint the kind of human beings to boast about. They just aint nothing like our kind of folks, and there's no getting used to them. Back up there in Beaseley County there's been plenty of times when the storekeepers argued and fussed about what we already owed on the books, but dogbite my pecker if they didn't always get around to letting us have what we wanted in the end, anyhow. And of course the next time I spoke about getting a little something on credit, the argument started all over again where it'd left off, but it always ended up with me getting what I wanted like I set out to do at the start. The storekeepers down here, though, won't even let you start an argument. And the Chinamen, who you'd think would be tickled to squealing to do business with a man like me, start jabbering like jaybirds in some strange tongue like they can't understand the common language that everybody else talks in. At a time like that it makes me feel like I aint wanted down here in this part of the world. I reckon I just wasn't born to go no farther from home than I can hollo."

Maud sighed wearisomely and turned over on her side, pressing her thin face against the wall. It had been almost a week since she had had the taste of tonic in her mouth, and almost that long since she had been on her feet to walk about the house. When she was first stricken with chills-and-fever, a clerk in a drug store had sold her a box of red pills which he promised would cure her. She took all the pills in the box, but at the end of a week she was no better than she had been before taking them, and so she began dosing herself with the tonic. Since early that spring when the chills-and-fever started, she had taken Dr. Munday's as often as she could get a bottle. The tonic had failed to cure the chills-and-fever, but nonetheless within a short time after drinking a quarter-bottle, or more, she always felt as good as she had ever felt in her life; and the sensation, which generally lingered for three or four hours, was one of the few pleasures in life she was capable of indulging in. The only thing she liked better was drinking a whole bottle at a time, but the cost was discouraging. They had to pay sixty-nine cents for a dollar-size bottle at the cut-rate drug stores.

"Maud, I done the best I could," Spence said comfortingly. He placed his hand on her chest and moved it over the feverish skin. "Maybe by tomorrow I can figure out a way to get you a bottle."

Maud said nothing. She knocked his hand away with her elbow and drew her knees up against her chest and

8

pulled the damp quilt over her body. The cot began to tremble as the chills shook her violently. Spence stood up.

The music coming from the next room stopped abruptly with a loud piercing wail, and Spence hurried to the door. He bent forward, pressing his ear against the crack, and listened. He could not detect a sound of any kind in the next room, and he began to wonder if he had fooled himself into thinking that Libby had come home for a visit. As he thought about it, he told himself that Maud had not said a word about Libby's being there; Maud could have turned the radio on herself, for that matter. The music started again and, with another dance tune filling his ears, Spence opened the door and walked in.

The shades had been drawn over the windows, and at first he could see only the dim shadowy outline of the room. He went forward several steps and stopped.

"Libby?" he called apprehensively. He held his breath while he waited for her to answer. "Libby!" he called again. By that time he realized he could not even hear the sound of his own voice above the music coming from the radio. He went to the nearest window and pulled back the shade. "Libby! What in the world—" he said, reaching for the radio.

Without taking his eyes from her, he found the knob and switched off the music.

"What's going on, Libby?" he asked slowly.

He went to the foot of the bed.

"Papa! Get out!" she said crossly when she realized he was in the room. "Go on out, Papa!"

Spence's mouth fell open as he stared at her. She was

9

in bed with a man who had a long purple scar on his shoulder that looked like a bayonet wound. As Spence leaned over the foot of the bed and stared at him, he was surprised to see that the man's face looked familiar. He appeared to be about twenty-five years old, or at least several years older than Libby, who was twenty, and he had thick muscular shoulders and a broad weather-tanned face. The purple skin over the wound was thin and transparent, looking as if it had only recently healed. He looked up at Spence and smiled friendlily. Spence stared back at him uncertainly. He did not know whether to smile at him or to scowl. It was the first time he had ever seen Libby in bed with a man. He chewed the tip of his tongue, wondering what to say.

"Papa, please go on out!" Libby said uneasily.

Spence leaned over the foot of the bed and peered searchingly at the boy's grinning face.

"It's Jim Howard Vance!" Spence shouted gleefully. He went around the corner of the bed in two strides. "Dogbite it if it aint! Where in the world did you come from, Jim boy?"

He slapped Jim Howard on the back several times and then grabbed him by the thick growth of wiry black hair on his head. He shook the boy playfully.

"What you doing here, Jim boy?" he demanded excitedly.

"Papa!" Libby said sharply. She leaned over Jim Howard and tried to push Spence away. Spence paid no attention to her. "Papa, go on out like I tell you!" she cried desperately, hitting at him with her fists. "Now, get out!"

10

"Aint this something, to be running into you here like this, Jim boy?" Spence said, ignoring Libby and shaking Jim Howard by the hair. "I aint seen you since they drafted you into the army just before we left Beaseley County. I didn't know what had become of you."

"Papa!" Libby said angrily. "Get out of here!"

"Why?" Spence asked, holding up his elbow in order to ward off her blows. "What makes you act this way, Libby?"

"Because," she said. "Now, get out!"

"Well, I want to see Jim Howard," he retorted, sitting down on the edge of the bed. "Where've you been all this time, Jim boy? The last time I heard anything about you, they said you was missing somewhere in the war. Nobody ever expected to see you again after that."

"I got picked up on the battlefield a little late," he said, smiling at Spence. "I didn't think anybody'd see me again, either. But they brought me back over here and put me in a hospital where they've been working on me for quite a while. I'm pretty well patched up now."

Spence slapped him resoundingly on the back.

"Dogbite it, Jim boy, I wouldn't take anything for seeing you again! I hate to see you all scarred up like that on your shoulder, but I reckon it's lucky you got that kind of a reminder, which'll fade away as time goes on, instead of being killed and buried over there in one of them faraway countries among all them strange people. . . . What you doing 'way down here so far from home, though? Why aint you back up there in Beaseley County?"

"I'm going to get a medical discharge in a few days, and believe me that's where——"

"Jim Howard's got to be back at the hospital very soon, Papa," Libby spoke up. "You can talk to him some other time. Please, Papa!"

Spence leaned back, his squinting black eyes watching them sharply.

"Now, look here!" he said. "Have you two gone and got married?"

Jim Howard and Libby glanced at one another.

"Well, did you?" Spence demanded insistently.

Jim Howard thrust a hand over his shoulder and scratched his back. Libby was squirming uncomfortably beside him.

"Not exactly, Papa," Libby said finally. "I mean, not completely. We got the license, but that took up so much time we decided we'd better wait——"

Jim Howard leaned over the side of the bed and extracted an official-looking paper from his pants pocket. He held the paper up for Spence to see. Spence blinked his eyes.

"Wait for what?" Spence asked Libby. "What's there to wait for when you're getting married?"

"We didn't have time to do everything the same day, Papa. We couldn't get the license and go through the ceremony and do everything else, too. Jim Howard's got to hurry back!"

"Hurry back where?"

"Back to the government hospital."

"What for?"

12

"Don't you understand anything at all, Papa!" she said crossly. "He's not supposed to be out of the hospital until he gets his discharge. He slipped out for a few hours so we could get the marriage license, and he's got to be back before they miss him. If they found out he had slipped away, they might never give him the discharge."

Spence moved his head up and down with a slow deliberate motion. He wanted to be agreeable in the presence of company, but he still could not understand why Libby was much less concerned than he was about the unperformed marriage ceremony. She was the one member of the family who had always respected the conventions of life.

"I'm going to get my discharge in two or three days if all goes well," Jim Howard told him. "As soon as I get it, it'll only take a few minutes for a preacher to marry us. Then, everything'll be taken care of, pop."

"Then what's going to happen?" Spence asked.

"Then we're going up to Beaseley County," he said. "And that's what you ought to do, too. This aint no place for you. It looks to me like you'd have found that out by now. That's why I was in such a hurry for me and Libby to get married. I don't want her coming anywhere near a place like this. And she won't, neither, because I'm taking her back to Beaseley County."

"Folks has to live some place, Jim boy," Spence protested. "Some has to live here, some other places."

"Maybe so, but they don't have to live like people do in Poor Boy," Jim Howard said firmly. "When I got

13

called up to the army, I kicked like a mule, because I wanted to stay put where I was in Beaseley County. But they sent me traveling all over the country, and then over there to England and to Africa and to Italy, and now I'm glad about it because I had my eyes opened so wide they almost popped out of my head. People don't have to live all their lives in a dump like this, being down and out, and ragged and hungry. I sure am glad the war came when it did, because if it hadn't, I'd never have known there was a good way to live—as well as a bad."

No one moved for several moments. Then Spence felt his daughter's hands pushing him away from the bed.

"Now, quit that shoving, Libby," Spence said angrily. "Just because Jim Howard had himself a long say aint no reason for thinking I aint thinking of a thing or two to tell him."

"Oh, shut up and get out!" she cried impatiently. "I'm old enough to know what I'm doing!"

"That's just it!" Spence shouted. "I wasn't going to mention it in the face of company, but you know too much for somebody who aint completely married yet. Jim Howard may be just like a member of the family, but if you aint all the way married, then he aint enough of the family to be in bed with you. You know yourself you're making it 'way too easy, even if it is for a soldier wounded in the war."

Libby sprang to her feet and, before he could stop her, pushed him out of the room. The bolt clicked in the lock, and a moment later he could hear the sound of her bare feet as she ran back to bed.

14

CHAPTER TWO

SPENCE WENT TO THE CLOSED DOOR AND tried the knob several times. The radio was switched on again, and he realized he would never make himself heard above the sound. He knew he could break the lock, but he was afraid to do that, because if Libby became any more angry than she was, she might go away and not come back. No matter what happened, he did not want her to leave. She always cooked his meals for him when she was there for a visit, and ever since he had heard the radio while walking home beside the canal, he had been looking forward to the hot meal she would cook him that night.

He left the door and went to the kitchen for a drink of water. While he waited for the water to run cool, he tried to think of some way of getting into the room so he could talk to Jim Howard. He felt that he had to talk to somebody about Beaseley County. It had been almost three years since he had talked to anybody from home, and there were times when his homesickness was so intense that he did not believe he could keep on living any longer. Maud wanted to go back to Beaseley County just as much as he did, but she had her chills-and-fever to keep her mind occupied, and she spent most of the time complaining because she could not get enough tonic. It was different with him, though. He was almost fifty years old, and it worried him to think that he might die down there and be buried in the pauper's cemetery along with all the others who could not afford to have their bodies shipped back home in a coffin. During the past year several men he knew had died in Poor Boy, and every one of them had been stranded there like he was. The wife of one of the men had tried to raise enough money to ship the remains back to his old home. When Spence was asked to contribute something, he had said that if a man could not raise enough money to ship himself home alive, he should not expect neighbors to ship him back dead, but he had been worried about himself ever since.

Still worrying about what would happen to him if he died away from home, he left the kitchen and went to the back porch to sit in the cool of the day while waiting for Jim Howard to come out of Libby's room.

It was about an hour until sunset, and the balmy breeze blowing inland from the Gulf felt good after the hot day he had spent walking the streets. From where he sat, with his feet on the porch railing, he could see barges and oil tankers, and occasionally a heavily loaded ocean freighter, move leisurely down the canal to the Gulf of Mexico. It had been a little less than three years since he had moved down there from Beaseley County to work for wartime wages in the powder plant. But the powder plant had been closed for nearly a year, and he was stranded, jobless, and homesick. He had worked for a while at the cotton compress plant on the other side of the canal, but that job had lasted only a few weeks. When he was laid off, the foreman had told him he was too weak for the work and that a strong Negro would be hired to take his place. After that, he had been unable to find a steady job anywhere in the whole city. For a while he had hired out to do odd jobs by the hour, but as time went on he had found out that there were fewer and fewer things he had the strength to do, and the constant walking in search of work tired him out before he could find anybody to hire him. Now he owed house rent for two months, and in a few days a third month's rent would fall due. Libby had a job in the city but, even though the few dollars a week she contributed to their support kept them from going hungry part of the time, her earnings were not large enough to pay the house rent in addition to her own living expenses.

Spence got up to go to the front of the house where he would be certain to see Jim Howard when he left Libby's room. He was half-way to the door before he realized that somebody was walking out on the porch. He stopped, hesitated for a moment, and backed against the railing. A strange woman, middle-aged and forbidding in appearance, was looking at him with a cold steady gaze. She was wearing a small black hat that looked as if it had been made for a man, a dark gray jacket and skirt, thick black stockings, and broad-toed low-heel shoes. Spence stared at her in amazement, looking her up and down time after time while he tried to think who she could be.

"You are Spencer Douthit," she stated, the tone of her voice sounding to Spence as though he were being accused of being who he was. "That's correct, isn't it?"

"It aint nothing else," he managed to say, looking her up and down once more. "How'd you know it?"

"Never mind how I knew," she said crisply.

Spence nodded obediently in the presence of such an awesome human being.

"I am Mrs. Jouett," the woman said, watching Spence as though she dared him to contradict her.

"You are?" he said, nodding.

Mrs. Jouett raised her chin higher, looking as though she were getting ready to sniff an obnoxious odor, and inspected Spence's back yard with a sweeping glance.

"I've just walked through your house," she said. "I must say I'm not a bit surprised."

"Surprised at what?"

"At the condition of your living quarters."

"I didn't know it was anybody's business——"

"I make such things my business," she interrupted.

"How come you can do that?" he asked. "If I went around sticking my nose in other folks'——"

"That's beside the point," she broke in. "Now, just look at this place!" she said, sweeping her arm in a wide arc. "Don't you people in this neighborhood take any pride in your surroundings? Why don't you pick up all those rusty tin cans and filthy beer bottles?"

Spence turned around and glanced at the cans and bottles strewn over his yard. He had become so accustomed to seeing the litter that he had forgotten all about it.

"I reckon it takes so much time stirring around for something to eat that there aint no time left for nothing else," he said. "But I would pick up them old cans and bottles if I had a place to dump them. I used to throw them in the canal over there, but the police came around one time and put a stop to that."

For a moment she looked as if she were on the verge of saying something to him, but instead she shook her head and walked into the house. Spence followed her inside. She was surveying the disordered kitchen when he caught up with her.

"I'm assigning a field worker to your case, Mr. Douthit," she said in a sharp tone.

"What's this you're doing?" he asked, puzzled.

"I'm sending a field worker here to take over this case. And I hope we don't have any trouble with you."

"I wasn't even studying about making trouble," he protested.

"Then see to it that you don't," she warned him.

Mrs. Jouett turned on her heel and strode through the house, her heavy strides jarring the building, until she came to the corner where Maud lay perspiring under the quilt. She pulled back the cover and looked at Maud's damp body.

"Who's that?" she asked.

"Why, that's my wife."

Mrs. Jouett dropped the quilt and stepped back.

"What's wrong with her?"

"She's just ailing, that's all."

"Have you had a doctor here to see her?"

"She aint bad off enough yet for that."

Mrs. Jouett turned sharply on her heel and went to the front porch. Spence followed her curiously.

"You have a daughter named Mavis," she said, briskly flipping the pages of a small notebook. "The child is thirteen years old."

"That's the first time anybody's called her that in I don't know how long," Spence said. "Mavis is a big grown girl now. She just shot up overnight."

He watched Mrs. Jouett flip through the notebook, wondering if she were selling something that a thirteen-year-old girl would want. She looked at several pages before closing the notebook with a flourish. Then she looked up and glared at Spence accusingly.

"Why don't you go to work and provide a decent home for your family?" she demanded of him.

Spence was unable to speak right away. His lips twitched nervously while he tried to think of something to say to a strange woman who would ask such a question. He thought everybody knew about his troubles, and it made him angry to have Mrs. Jouett, or anyone like her, come to his house uninvited and talk to him in that manner.

"Maybe you don't know it," he said calmly, "but there's plenty of people in this world who have a hard time eking out a living, and I figure I'm one of them. I'd like to be well-off as much as the next man to come along, but it just won't work out for me that way. I was born poor, and I'll die poor, and I won't be nothing but poor in between. Now, there aint no sense in you coming around here and trying to tell me otherwise."

"Nonsense!" Mrs. Jouett said impatiently. "There's no excuse for a man to be down and out in these days and times. I have no sympathy for a man who won't go out and get himself a job."

Spence's lips tightened across his teeth and he held his breath for several moments.

"The folks who begged people like me to leave home and come down here ought to be made to take the blame for what's happened," he said angrily. "They're the ones who pestered me about coming down here and working in the war plants. I moved down here nearly three years ago to work in the powder plant, and you know good and well that plant aint been running for nearly a year. They've stripped all the machinery out of it and shipped it off somewhere else, and that's why it aint never going to run again so I can get me a job."

"I had nothing whatsoever to do with that," Mrs. Jouett snapped. "You should have stayed at home, anyway."

"Stayed at home!" Spence repeated. "How could anybody stay at home in those days with them round-up men rip-snorting through the country handing out big bottles of whiskey to the men and black lace drawers to the womenfolks? If it'd just been me, I could've drunk their liquor and thought nothing of it, but you know yourself that there aint nothing else in the world that can get a woman stirred up like fancy drawers. And then of course the bourbon and black lace drawers stopped as soon as we got down here and went to work, and I aint seen them round-up fellows since. I reckon they're off somewhere else getting folks upset and sending them to some other big city to suffer like I'm doing."

"You didn't have to come down here," she said.

"No, but they said it was the patriotic thing to do."

"Well, it's just as patriotic now to go back where you came from."

"Dogbite it, woman, what in hell do you think I've been trying to do every day for the past whole year!"

"It is a pity the powder plant ever closed down," she admitted, nodding to Spence as though she were compelled to agree with him to that extent.

"If you ask me, I'd say it's a pity it ever started up in the first place," Spence said heatedly. "If it hadn't, then them big-city round-up fellows wouldn't have come tearing through Beaseley County day and night waving them black lace drawers at the womenfolks and showing them how to try them on. I came home one time and caught two of them in the front yard. They'd already got Libby rigged out in a pair, and one of them was showing Maud how to button them on. The worst part about it, though, was that after those boosters got my wife all dolled-up, they made her promise not to take them off till I agreed to come down here and work in the plant. I held out one whole day and part of the night before I'd say I'd sign the little slip of paper and draw the train tickets, but by that time I was feeling like a rabbit with his balls caught in a sewingmachine, and I just couldn't hold out no longer. That's a mean low-down trick to play on a man, if you ask me, and it was the cause of the whole mess I'm in right now."

"I have no more time to talk to you," Mrs. Jouett said conclusively, turning away and going down the steps to the yard. She began walking rapidly towards the street, but suddenly she stopped and turned around. "By the way, Mr. Douthit," she called, "what kind of a job did you have at the powder plant?"

"It wasn't much to brag about," Spence said.

"But I want to know," she insisted. "What did you do?"

"Well, I sat on a stool beside a little trough that had something that smelled like rotten eggs and looked like sulphur and molasses running through it. Every fifteen minutes a bell went *clang-clang-clang* and a red light flashed on. Then I jumped up and blew a whistle and took a dipperful of the stuff and poured it in a bottle. After that I sat down and waited another fifteen minutes to do it all over again."

"Why did you blow a whistle?"

"Oh, they said that was to wake me up so I'd pour the stuff in the bottle instead of down my throat."

"And that's all you did at the powder plant?"

"That's every lick. But it got tiresome after a while. If I'd known a trade, like carpentering or barbering or the like, there was many a day when I'd have walked right away from that job. That work was just too tiresome for only sixty-two-fifty a week."

"The field worker will be here shortly, Mr. Douthit," she said as she turned and hurried away.

CHAPTER THREE

CHET MITCHELL, WHO WAS A LARGE RED-faced man of forty-two, and whose loud raucous voice could be heard from one end of the street to the other, came out on his back porch and hung his razor-strop on a post. When Spence heard him whistling, he strolled to the back of the house where he would be in a position to order Chet back into his own yard if he stepped over the imaginary line dividing the two lots.

The two houses, like all the dwellings on that side of the street, were identical in construction and appearance. Each one contained three rooms, including the kitchen, and there were front and rear porches. The houses, which were about twenty-five years old, had rented for as much as thirty-five dollars a month when money was plentiful, but now the owner, who lived in a twenty-room brick house in a northern suburb of the city, was content to get fifteen. The lots were narrow and the buildings only eight feet apart: but the rent was cheap, and those who could afford it felt superior to the other people in Poor Boy who lived in squatters' shacks along the canal. All the houses were shabby and in need of repair, however, and once when Spence spoke to the rent collector about replacing the broken glass in his windows, the collector had laughed at him and said that the house was plenty good enough as it was for people who could afford nothing better. After that Spence did not think it was worthwhile to complain about the leaky roof and the corner of the house that had slipped off the foundation.

Spence sat down on the back porch and watched Chet, who was then standing only ten feet away, from the corners of his eyes. He had not spoken to Chet since Mavis, his younger daughter, ran away from home, and he had no intention of doing so now. Spence had always disliked Chet. He disliked him because Chet was bigger and stronger than he was, because Chet always had plenty of money in his pocket, and because every time they got into an argument he was shouted down by Chet's bellowing husky voice.

Chet took off his shirt and began stropping the razor. He was the one person who lived in Poor Boy by preference and not by necessity. Everyone knew that Chet made his living, and a good one at that, by selling marijuana, which he bought in large quantities, to pool room and cocktail lounge peddlers. The police never bothered Chet. He paid a fairly large sum of money monthly to somebody in the city, which was his permit to sell as many marijuana cigarettes as his peddlers could dispose of. The only time Chet had been in trouble was when he once forgot to make a monthly payment. That night two men followed him home, shoved pistols into his stomach, and asked him if he knew what day it was. Chet paid up in a hurry and the men left.

Myrt brought a basin of hot water from the kitchen and put it on the shelf at the corner of the porch. Chet lathered his face and began to shave. Myrt watched him, fascinated, while he shaved one side of his face. Neither one of them said anything but, as she turned to go back into the kitchen, Chet suddenly reached down and poked her on her stomach with his finger, at the same time making a loud sucking-sound with his lips. Myrt screamed, slapped at him playfully, and ran into the house. Spence found himself jumping nervously out of his chair at the sound of Myrt's scream as though he had been tickled instead of her. Chet cocked his head to one side and looked over at Spence inquiringly.

"You still here, hillbilly?" Chet said in his loud voice. "I thought you said you was leaving town. Didn't you say that about six months ago? What's holding you up?"

Spence tried his best to ignore Chet. He looked straight ahead and gritted his teeth. He could hear Chet laugh, and a moment later he began whistling again. After he had finished shaving, he wiped the razor, dried his face, and hung the towel on the porch railing. Spence watched him from the corners of his eyes, being careful to keep his face turned straight ahead. Still whistling, Chet picked up the basin and threw the soapy water directly into Spence's yard. Then he waited, whistling louder than ever. to find out what Spence was going to do about it.

27

Spence leaped to his feet, glaring first at the puddle of water and then at Chet.

"Anybody who'd empty his slop in another man's yard ought to be made to get down and lick it up!" Spence shouted angrily. Chet, who weighed two hundred and thirty pounds, was laughing so much his belly shook. "And if I was anywhere near your size, Chet Mitchell, I'd be the one to make you do it, too!"

Chet leaned over the railing, still shaking with laughter, and Myrt came to the kitchen door for a moment to see what had happened.

"Don't you know if you keep your yard damp it'll make fishing-worms grow in it, hillbilly?" Chet said. "A man like you ought to keep plenty of fishing-worms on hand all the time."

"I aint no hillbilly, and you know it!" Spence said, raising his voice as loud as he could.

"Hell, I've been through Beaseley County," Chet said, "and I know what it's like up there. It's the God-forsakenest place I ever hope to see. The people up there are so poor they wouldn't know what to do with a dollar-bill if they found one in the big road. All them hills and gullies give me nightmares every time I think about it."

"It's just like any other good part of the world," Spence said defensively. "People like you from this flat country down here think every little rise of ground is a big hill. Beaseley County is God's own country."

"Well, you and God can have it, then," Chet said. "But I sure do pity anybody who has to make a living out of

28

them stony fields. I wouldn't wish that country on the meanest man in town."

"I'm going to get even with you!" Spence said threateningly after a pause. "You just wait and see if I don't. I'll get even with you if it takes a lifetime."

"How you going to do that, hillbilly?"

"That's for you to find out when it's too late to stop it. But whatever it is, it'll be good and plenty. Nobody's going to do to a daughter of mine what you done, and not get paid back. If it wasn't for you, she wouldn't have got the notion in her head to run off. You're to blame for it, and I ought to have the law on you. And I might still do it, too!"

Chet jumped off the porch and ran to Spence's steps. Spence stood his ground.

"I've heard enough of that whining!" Chet said loudly, his face becoming redder than ever. "You aint going to stand there and blame me for that and get away with it. If I hadn't done it, somebody else would have before the week was out. She was ripe, and you know it. Besides, she came over there to my house. I didn't come over here to yours, did I? You've got to give me credit for that!"

"Just the same, you could've let nature take its course," Spence said. "It was a mean low-down thing to do, at her age. Now she's gone off, running wild all over the city, and can't nothing stop her."

"You know good and well everybody in this part of town had his eyes on her. If there was one, there was a dozen just itching for the chance. Even a blind man could tell she was wanting to be jumped. I aint going to be blamed for taking the first opportunity just because she lived next door to me. Now, that's final!"

Chet left the steps and started for his own yard, glancing back over his shoulder to make sure that Spence was not picking up a rock to throw at him. He went as far as the imaginary line dividing the two lots.

"It's people like you who ought to be made to go back where you came from," Spence shouted at him. "I don't know where you came from, but they ought to send you back to Tennessee or Alabama or wherever it was."

"I'm staying here for the next ten years, just like I've been here for the past ten years. Why in hell don't you go back where you came from? Nobody wants you around here!"

"I'm leaving, but I'll leave when I'm ready, and of my own accord."

"You'll be hanging around here until you die, unless somebody sends you away," Chet said, laughing sneeringly. "I've seen no-accounts like you from them hills before, sitting on your tails and bellyaching because the world won't come around and give you a living. This whole town's over-run with people like you who don't have the sense to know you aint wanted here no more. By God, if I was running things it'd be different. I'd get me a good strong mule whip and start swinging it. You'd either high-tail it back to them hills, or you'd get your brains beaten out!"

Chet spat across the line into Spence's yard and went into his house to eat supper. Spence was on the verge of going to Chet's door and telling him what he thought of him when he heard the screendoor slam behind him. He turned around and saw Libby crossing the porch.

"Where's Jim Howard?" he asked anxiously, running up the steps to her.

"He had to leave, Papa," she said. "He couldn't stay another minute."

His face sagged with disappointment.

"But, you said——"

"I know, Papa, but it was so late I was afraid he'd get into trouble at the hospital."

She crossed the porch to the low stool and sat down to gaze over the weed-grown vacant lots between them and the canal. The sun was going down in a huge red fire, and its glowing rays tinted everything they touched. Spence walked past her and sat down in the chair at the railing. He felt that he had been cheated, and he turned to her angrily.

"I think it was a mean thing to do," he said.

Libby patted his hand and smiled at him.

"Now, Papa," she said appealingly.

He could not be angry with her after that, and he found himself nodding his head with forgivingness. She had always been a beautiful girl, even long before they left Beaseley County, but he had never seen her look so lovely before. Her dark hair was blue-black, and her slender body was round and firm. Spence gazed at her admiringly. Maud had been almost as beautiful when she was twenty.

"Now, look here, Libby," he said loudly. "I aint for-got about the way you shoved me around just a while

31

ago. That was a persnickity thing to do, and you know it. I'm your daddy, and I've got a right to speak up when I catch you in bed with a man. I know all you said about getting married, but just the same you really aint."

"We are going to," she said calmly.

"Going to!" he said, raising his voice. "What's the use of going to, when you and him was in bed like that? When you do what you was doing, there aint nothing else left to do! I've seen some sights in my time, but I never thought I'd come home and find you——"

"Don't forget, Papa. We have a marriage license. That's a lot more than some girls ever get."

"I reckon you're right about that," he admitted. "Besides that, Jim Howard Vance is a pretty smart fellow. He was talking in there just a while ago like he knows a thing or two. There's not many I'd want to trust between the time of taking out a license and using it, but Jim Howard's not one of them. If he says he's going to marry you, I believe him."

Libby was silent. He turned and saw her looking at the sunset. The warm golden light sparkled in her eyes.

Spence waited until the sun sank out of sight before disturbing her. When he touched her arm, she turned with a startled motion. He could see tears clinging to her eyes.

"What's the matter, Libby?"

She dropped her head on his shoulder, pressing her warm damp face against him.

"It's so awful, Papa," she said brokenly. "We're just

32

the same as married, but Jim Howard had to go away so soon. If he could only have stayed tonight . . ."

Spence turned his head away from her as she sobbed against his shoulder. He gazed at the canal while his rough hand stroked her hair. It reminded him of the first time he held Maud in his arms and tried to comfort her. Maud was young like Libby then, and on their wedding day when the sun went down and darkness closed around them, Maud cried like a baby and wanted to go home to her parents.

An oil tanker was moving slowly down the canal to the Gulf, its lights twinkling like stars against the pale sky. Spence watched the tanker until it was out of sight. After that a tug, puffing clouds of black smoke and pushing an empty barge, labored up the canal towards the slips a mile away. Spence felt Libby's hand squeezing his.

"It'll be all right," she was saying in a low voice. "In two or three days he'll be discharged, and he'll come for me, and then everything will be different, and we'll go away. He's been away nearly two years, and I've waited that long for him, and I can wait two or three days longer. It's not like it would be if he'd been killed in the war. He's here. He didn't get killed. We'll be together for the rest of our lives . . . Two more days . . . or three more, and we'll be going up to Beaseley County. Then all this will be over. I won't have to wait for him another second. We'll be going home. . . ."

Spence felt his body tremble with anxiety.

"But what about the rest of us, Libby?" he asked fearfully. "What about your Ma and me? You know we aint got a dime to live on, except what you give us. And what about Mavis? She's off somewhere, all on account of that Chet Mitchell over there, and she won't come back. It just wouldn't be right for you to go away. Now, if I was the only one to consider, I could go along with you and Jim Howard to Beaseley County. But it wouldn't seem right if I went off and left Mavis and your Ma down here to scramble for themselves."

Libby sat up and dried her tears. Spence could see the expression on her face change almost immediately.

"Jim Howard's right, Papa," she said in an even voice. "You've got to get away from this terrible place and take Ma and Mavis with you. There's no excuse for staying here any longer. You can find Mavis if you'll go out and look for her, and you can sell the furniture for enough money for the bus fare home. I can't give you and Ma any more money after I stop working in town and go away with Jim Howard. You'll have to do something yourself from then on."

"But everybody knows I can't find me a job, Libby," Spence protested. "I just aint got the strength in my body to tussle with a thing like that no more."

"There are plenty of things you could do if you really want to go back to Beaseley County. Sometimes I think you don't want to leave Poor Boy, no matter what you say."

"That's a peculiar string of words to put together, Libby. Where in the world did you get a notion like that? I think Beaseley County is the finest spot in the land, and I don't hesitate to say so, neither!"

34

"Maybe you do think that, but you know life's a lot easier down here. If you went back up there, you'd have to farm in summer and cut wood in winter. Down here you don't have to do a blessed thing as long as somebody comes around every week and hands you a few dollars."

"I declare, Libby, you get the queerest notions some-times——"

"It's about time you started thinking about some of those queer notions," she said, getting up and standing before him at the railing. Spence glanced up at her face. When he saw the harsh expression, he quickly lowered his gaze. "You can do something about it if you want to. And you'd better do something before it's too late."

Spence chewed the tip of his tongue. His mind was racing with worry. Presently he glanced up at his daughter.

"Maybe every word you say is God's own truth, Libby," he told her, "but maybe if you waited a year or so, things would get better around here, and then I'd have me a good little job and you could go ahead and marry Jim Howard. I'll bet a pretty he'll wait that long, and in the meanwhile you could keep your job in the city so there'd be a few dollars coming in for your Ma and me."

"I'm afraid that wouldn't do, Papa," she said with a laugh. "A man will wait for a girl just so long, but no longer. There are too many others ready to marry him."

She left him and went to the kitchen door.

"It's time to cook supper, isn't it, Papa?"

"We're short on coffee," Spence said, leaping to his

35

feet. "I've been boiling the old grounds for the past three days."

Libby unfastened the front of her dress and took out several greenbacks.

"Your Ma needs some tonic bad, Libby," he suggested, watching her unfold the money. "And I'm out of tobacco, too."

She gave him five dollars.

"We need food more than tonic or tobacco," she told him. "Remember that when you get down to the stores."

"Oh, I'll get that," he promised. "With all this money to spend, I'll stock up for sure. Now, you get the stove hot, and I'll be back in no time."

He ran down the steps and hurried to the street. It was a quarter of a mile to the small group of stores, but he knew several short-cuts across vacant lots that saved a lot of time when he was in a hurry. There were no other stores in Poor Boy, with the exception of half-a-dozen small soft-drink and tobacco stands scattered over the neighborhood, and the main business section of the South Side was a mile away. The city itself lay spread over miles of the flat land, and as he trotted through the dark unlit streets he could see the lights in the north reflected in the sky like a lingering sunset.

Before buying anything else with the money, Spence got half-a-dozen packages of smoking tobacco at the drug store. He was afraid if he waited too long all the money would be spent for food.

He was half-way home when he remembered about Maud's tonic. All the money had been spent, though, and there was nothing he could do but go home without it.

Libby came to the back door when he called her. The kitchen was lighted, and he could see a hot fire glowing in the cook-stove grate.

"I got all the groceries, Libby," he said, panting with exertion as he handed her the packages. "The big trouble is that I bought so much to eat I didn't have a dime left over for your Ma's tonic. She's going to be awfully upset if she don't get some tonight."

Libby carried the packages to the table without a word. When she came back to the door, she handed him a dollar.

"You didn't forget to buy some tobacco, did you, Papa?" she asked without a smile.

"No," he said slowly, watching her face. "Why?"

"Because that dollar is all you're going to get," she said as she turned around and went back into the kitchen.

All the way down to the drug store Spence was tempted to go to Bill Tarrant's private club and try to double the dollar. However, when he got to the store, he was tired and hungry, and he knew he could not go back to the house that night if he lost the dollar in a crap game. The last time he had tried to double money at Bill Tarrant's club, fully expecting to win, he had lost on the first roll of the dice. As hungry as he was then, he did not feel it was worth the risk this time. He went into the drug store and bought a large-size bottle of tonic, spending the change for more smoking tobacco.

When he got back to the house, he went straight to the bedroom to wake up Maud. She was still facing the

37

wall when he turned on the light, but the chills had passed and she had kicked off the quilt. He held the bottle before her eyes tantalizingly and watched her reach for it. Spence drew it from her reach as she sat up wild-eyed with surprise. She began whimpering like a child begging for candy, crying and laughing at the same time.

"I take back every hateful thing I ever said, Spence," she said excitedly as she watched the bottle.

Spence opened the bottle and poured some of the tonic into a glass. Then he held it at arm's length, still beyond her reach. Tears were running down her cheeks.

"I didn't really think all those bad things, Spence! I knew you'd find a way to get Dr. Munday's for me!"

Spence sat down on the side of the cot and gave her the glass. She thrust it to her mouth and, cooing with delight, drank the last drop.

"It's the big dollar-size one, Maud," he told her, holding up the bottle for her to gaze upon. "It's the first big one you've had in a long time, aint it? All the others lately was those measely little fifty-cent bottles."

"Thank the Good Lord, Spence!" she muttered through trembling lips, still gasping for breath. She licked the rim of the glass. "I don't know what on earth I'd do without Dr. Munday's." She lay down on her back and smiled up at him while she dried the tears from her eyes and cheeks with the backs of her hands. "It's the one thing that keeps me alive."

Spence patted her shoulder and placed the bottle on the floor beside the cot where she could reach it easily.

"Now, to tell the truth, Maud, it was Libby who paid

38

for it," he admitted. "She gave me the dollar to buy it with. All I done was go get it."

"Bless her heart," Maud breathed appreciatively. She closed her eyes and a contented smile came to her face as the warmth of the liquid spread through her body. "It aint everybody who's got a thoughtful daughter who brings Dr. Munday's in the big bottle." She reached out her arm, wiggling her fingers in the direction of the bottle on the floor until Spence placed it in her hand. She took a long noisy drink and thrust it back at Spence. "Bless her heart and hide both," she said, closing her eyes and breathing deeply. A blissful expression covered her face.

Spence sat beside her for several minutes and watched the corners of her mouth spread outward and upward with contentment.

Libby had set the table and there was a steaming big dish of browneyed peas waiting for him. He sat down and began eating hungrily, and Libby brought a pan of casing-stuffed country sausage and a bowl of hot grits to the table. Spence began eating as fast as he could, helping himself to more peas and grits with his free hand.

"I don't reckon there's no man alive who likes browneyes and hog sausage the way I do," he mumbled, looking up at Libby. "It's a pity you can't stay here all the time and just cook. If there's one thing in the whole wide world I miss, it's a big dish of hominy grits and hog sausage every morning. When you aint here, there just aint a bite to eat. Your Ma's always ailing, or fixing to, and she won't cook. I'd do it if I could get the hang of the thing, but I just can't. I come out here and piddle around, but it don't amount to nothing in the end. I make a little coffee, and that's about all."

Libby brought a pan of hot cornbread from the oven and placed it on the table. Spence helped himself to a large piece and filled his plate with browneyed peas.

"Down here in this corner of the world, a man's lucky if he gets just one good dish like these once in a while," he said, chewing a mouthful of sausage, cornbread, and browneyed peas. "And there's some people down here, they tell me, who never even heard about a single one of them. I can't understand what such folks find worthwhile eating, if it aint grits and browneyes. Life just wouldn't be worthwhile to me if I didn't get some of them every now and then."

He glanced up to see Libby staring past him. He took another mouthful of grits and sausage before stopping to find out what she was looking at so intently. Libby rose up from her chair.

"What's wrong, Libby?" he asked, reaching for another piece of cornbread.

She nodded behind him, and Spence finally turned around.

Maud was standing unsteadily in the doorway, smiling at no one in particular. The pink nightgown had slipped down to her waist, and she was feeling her breasts in search of it. She began to sway from side to side as she attempted to balance herself, and she almost fell over before putting out one of her hands and holding to the door for support. The tickling sensation of her fingers on her chest made her tremble, and the gown fell around her feet, almost tripping her. She stepped out of it and giggled.

Spence was spellbound by her behavior, but Libby went to her mother and tried to take her by the arm. Maud drew back and hit at her with her open hand. Libby dodged and ran back to the table.

"Now, look here, Maud," Spence said, getting up and grabbing at her arm, "you oughtn't be parading around here like this. Go on back to bed where you belong."

Maud swung her arm at him. Her open-palm hand hit him squarely on the side of the head, making his ear ring. He sat down quickly, shaking his head like a dog that had been doused with a bucket of water.

"That'll teach you to leave a lady be when she's feeling whorish," Maud told him, snapping her head at him with a solemn movement.

She watched Spence and Libby a while, and then she went towards the table, lifting her knees and stepping forward daintily. She paused half-way.

"I heard somebody talking about browneyed peas and hominy grits," she said, looking from one to the other. "That's what I want to hear about!" she yelled at the top of her voice. She paused while she flicked imaginary specks of dust from her chest and stomach with her finger. "If you're talking about browneyes and grits, then this must be Beaseley County. Is this here Beaseley County?" she giggled loudly. "Huh?"

"Libby, your Ma's gone and emptied that whole dollar-bottle of tonic," Spence said, shaking his head meaningfully. "She's tipsy, if I ever saw it before. Even a rabbit with his balls caught in a sewingmachine would know this place aint Beaseley County."

Maud tossed her head as though she had been unreasonably affronted. She turned and, feeling her way through the door with both hands, walked haughtily out of the kitchen.

CHAPTER FOUR

IT HAD TAKEN LIBBY AND SPENCE A LONG time to get Maud calmed down enough so she would stay in bed, and the sun was high over the housetops when Spence opened his eyes the next morning. Before the effects of the tonic had finally disappeared, though, Maud had managed to slip out of the house and go yelling down the street. When he caught up with her, she was banging her fists on a neighbor's front door, and Spence had to pin her arms to her side and drag her home. Maud's shouting and screaming woke up Chet and Myrt, and they came out on their porch to find out what the trouble was. Spence paid no attention to them when he carried Maud past their house, and they went back to bed. For an hour after that Maud had made life miserable by screaming and fighting, because she thought she was entitled to have a good time, and she insisted on having a party. Sometime after midnight Libby finally persuaded her to stay in bed, and soon after that she fell into heavy sleep.

43

Spence raised his head a few inches from the pillow and looked across the room at Maud. She was still asleep on her cot, and he lay awake for a long time listening to her heavy breathing. She had kicked the quilt off, and the nightgown was missing.

He dozed off to sleep again, but Chet Mitchell's loud voice woke him with a start. Chet was shouting at Myrt about something that displeased him, and Spence sat up and rubbed his eyes, knowing he could not go back to sleep after that. He listened to Chet for several minutes before it occurred to him to look at the door to the next room. The door was wide open, and almost immediately he felt a sickly sensation deep in his stomach. Libby had left.

Leaping out of bed, he trotted gingerly on his bare feet to the door. He did not have to go any farther to convince himself that Libby had gone. The bed was empty and there were none of her clothes in the room. He turned away heavy-heartedly and began looking for his pants and shirt.

While he was dressing he was certain he heard somebody splash a basin of water somewhere in the back yard, and he ran to the kitchen door. The first thing he saw was a puddle of soapy water midway between his doorstep and the corner of the porch. He pulled on his pants while he watched the water gradually soak into the ground. From the corners of his eyes he could see Chet watching him from his porch, and he walked to the railing and spat disgustedly at the puddle.

"You're a sorry neighbor, if there ever was one," he told Chet without looking at him.

Chet leaned against the post and laughed.

"What got into your old woman last night?" he asked after a while. "Can't you keep her tamed down, hill-billy?"

"I got along first-rate before I ever heard tell of you, Chet Mitchell, and I can keep on doing it, too."

"If you'll take my advice, you'll keep your old woman in the house," Chet said, "because if you don't, some-body's going to mistake her for a deer one of these nights and draw a bead on her." He reached down and picked up Maud's nightgown from a chair. He rolled the gar-ment into a tight ball and threw it at Spence. "I found that in my front yard this morning, hillbilly," he said.

Spence picked up the gown, spat at the puddle, and went into the kitchen.

There was a pan of freshly baked biscuits still warm in the stove, and a pot of coffee was made. Spence kin-dled the fire to heat the coffee and got the sorghum jug from the closet. There was a long piece of casing-stuffed sausage left over from supper, and he put that on the table, too. When he was ready to eat, he broke open half-a-dozen biscuits and poured sorghum over them.

The coffee was soon boiling, and Spence brought the pot to the table. By then he was ready for another help-ing of biscuits and sorghum, and he cut another piece of sausage.

He had just finished drinking the last of the coffee when he felt somebody touch his arm. He turned around,

45

thinking it was Maud, but he saw one of Floyd Sharp's little tow-headed girls standing at his elbow and watching him hungrily as he sopped up sorghum with a biscuit. The little girl was about five years old, but Floyd had so many little girls, all of whom looked alike to Spence, that he had never been able to tell them apart.

"Are you Clarice?" he asked of her, stuffing the sorghum and biscuit into his mouth.

She shook her head from side to side, her eyes fixed upon the biscuits and sorghum in his plate. Spence broke open a fresh biscuit, sopped up some sorghum with it, and handed it to the little girl. She took it eagerly, licking the dripping sorghum around the edges.

"Mr. Douthit, my name's Lillie Mae," she said, her big round eyes looking at him while she ate. "Clarice is my sister."

"I know that," he said, "but I just can't keep you girls straight in my mind. How many of you are there, now?"

"Mr. Douthit, I have seven sisters," she told him seriously. "Mamma says I will have a new baby sister, too."

She had eaten the biscuit and was licking her fingers. Spence gave her another piece with sorghum on it.

"Aint you had breakfast yet?" he asked, watching her eat hungrily.

"I had my breakfast, Mr. Douthit. We had grits."

"Why'd you come up here to my house?"

"Mr. Douthit, my daddy wants to know if you aint using your road map," she said hurriedly as though she were determined to remember what she had been told

46

to say, "and if you aint, can he borrow it for a little while?"

"What's your daddy want with it?" Spence asked anxiously. "Is he fixing to leave for home?"

"Mr. Douthit, we're not really going home. My daddy says he wants to look at the road map and pretend like we're going home."

"Oh," Spence said, relieved.

He poured sorghum on another piece of bread, handing it to Lillie Mae, and then helped himself to more sausage.

"This is as good as a sugar-tit, aint it, Mr. Douthit?" Lillie Mae said, licking the sorghum on her lips.

"I reckon it is!" he agreed. "I don't know much else that's better."

She waited quietly at the edge of the table, her hands locked tightly behind her back, and watched him finish eating.

"Mr. Douthit, are you going to give me your road map for my daddy?" she asked worriedly.

"I'll look around the house and see if I can find it anywhere," he told her. "When I find it, I'll bring it down to your house. I'm too busy to hunt for it right now."

"Good-bye then, Mr. Douthit," she said as she backed towards the door.

" 'Bye, Justine," he called out.

"I'm Lillie Mae," she corrected him promptly.

" 'Bye then, Lillie Mae," he said.

He could hear the pitty-pat of her small bare feet as she went through the house to the front porch. When the

47

screendoor slammed, he pushed back his chair and got up.

When he walked out on the back porch, the morning was almost over and the oppressive mid-day heat had settled down upon the earth. Chet had left home, and Myrt was sweeping the trash in their back yard. Spence leaned against a post and watched her interestedly. He never spoke to Myrt, unless he had a good reason for doing so, because he did not wish to have anything to do with some one so closely associated with Chet Mitchell. He and Chet had never been friendly, not even before the quarrel over Mavis came up, and for that reason Myrt was not forever running in and out of the house to visit Maud. Now, however, as he watched her stoop over and sweep the yard, Spence had the feeling that he could get friendly with her if he wanted to. He told himself that he would never get even with Chet if he did not begin looking around for some means of doing it. Myrt was a large woman with straw-colored hair and a ready smile. She was fairly good-looking, too. He had watched her many times when she ran out on the back porch thinking no one would see her.

Myrt turned around and looked at him for a moment. He was about to go down the steps and say something to her when he remembered that he still had not looked under Maud's pillow. That was more important than anything else just then.

He hurried into the house, tip-toeing noiselessly through the kitchen to the bedroom. Maud was sleeping soundly.

Going to the cot, Spence slipped his hand under her

48

pillow. Libby always put some money under her mother's pillow when she left, and Spence was certain there would be something there this time. He felt carefully under her head, doing his best to find the money without waking Maud. He was unable to find it the first time, and so he got down on his knees and slipped his hand inside the pillow-case once more. Just then Maud turned over and opened her eyes. She was awake in an instant. Before he could withdraw his hand, she slapped him and sat up.

"Where's Libby?" she asked, looking around the room.

Spence got up. He stood by the cot blaming himself for not finding the money before Maud woke up and caught him.

"Did Libby go away?" she said, putting her hand under the pillow and feeling for the money. After several moments she stopped searching for it and patted the pillow with a satisfied smile on her face. "Libby's gone," she announced.

Spence could do nothing but nod his head after that. Maud knew as well as he did that there would be no money under her pillow if Libby had not left.

"Libby cooked some fine hot biscuits before she went," Spence said, hoping Maud would get up and go to the kitchen. "Don't you want to go eat something, Maud?"

Maud patted the pillow and lay her head on it possessively. She watched Spence, saying nothing.

He waited a while longer to find out if Maud would change her mind and go to the kitchen, but she showed no signs of leaving the room as long as he was in it. He went to the box where he kept odds and ends and began looking for the road map. After taking everything from the box and scattering it on the floor, he found the map and put it into his hip pocket. On his way to the front porch he glanced at the cot, but Maud had not changed her position. He went down the steps and walked slowly toward Floyd Sharp's house.

Floyd was the best friend Spence had in Poor Boy. He was a few years younger than Spence, having reached his forty-fifth birthday that summer, but while Spence's hair was still bushy and black, Floyd's hair had turned gray. He always joked about his gray hairs, though, saying that any man who had eight daughters was lucky to have any hair left to turn gray. He had moved there at about the same time Spence did to work in the powder plant. Before the plant closed down, Floyd had lived in a rented house in the South Side; now he lived in a small two-room shack he had built himself on squatters' ground, and paid no rent.

Everyone gave Floyd credit for naming the neighborhood Poor Boy Town, because he had been the first to stake out rights and build a shack near the canal. Soon after that others who were jobless and unable to keep up their rent heard about Poor Boy and a year later several hundred families were living there. The ground was low and swampy, and after every heavy rain the water overflowed the creek and flooded yards and streets. The owners of most of the land considered it worthless, and the city had taken the greater part of it over for nonpayment of taxes. It was all part of the South Side, but the city, which sprawled for miles over the level country, was not much interested in Poor Boy. The people were impoverished, they could not pay taxes, and members of the city government did not need their votes in order to continue in office.

For the most part, the people who lived in Poor Boy were former powder plant workers who had been brought there from Arkansas, Tennessee, Mississippi, Alabama, and Georgia. Many of them had earned as much as a dollar and a half an hour for semi-skilled labor during the two years that the plant was in operation. No one in Poor Boy knew the reason why the plant was closed and its machinery shipped away. Some of the men argued that the plant was too far from either the Atlantic or Pacific coasts; others said that the government had built too many such plants. But whatever the reason was, there were hundreds of families stranded there now. The greater part of them had failed to save enough money to get them back to their homes; others did not have enough money to pay their bills so they could leave town. Pianos, radios, automobiles, and furniture had been sold piece by piece during the past year to raise money for food. Then, without a car, and with nothing left to sell, only the strongest-willed had been able to survive even in Poor Boy. Ten or twelve families had moved down the canal to the garbage dump where they spent their time sifting the rubbish and reclaiming unbroken bottles and scrap metal which they sold to junk dealers in the city. Both Floyd and Spence had vowed that they would rather starve than pick the garbage dump.

Floyd was sitting under the shadetree in his yard when

51

Spence waded through the rank growth of weeds surrounding his house. He looked up and waved. Three or four of Floyd's little girls ran out to meet Spence and followed him across the yard. It seemed to Spence that each time he came to visit Floyd, another toddling towhead had been added to his crowd. All of them were thin and hungry-looking, and none of them, with the exception of the oldest girl, seemed to grow any taller than a table-top. Floyd's wife, Bertha, always had a nursing baby in her arms.

"Mr. Douthit, gimme a penny," one of the little girls begged, pulling at Spence's pants-leg. "Please, Mr. Douthit!"

Spence waved the girl away and walked under the shadetree, taking off his hat and fanning his perspiring face. The girls clustered behind the tree and watched him curiously. Floyd waved them away. They scattered like a flock of chickens, but in a few moments they were back again.

"If it gets much hotter down here in Poor Boy," Spence said, fanning furiously, "I wouldn't be at all surprised to see the devil stick his head out of the ground one of these days and say he'd come to set up shop where the heat's hotter."

"That ain't no lie," Floyd agreed.

Floyd's oldest girl, Justine, came out of the house and walked towards the shadetree. She was twelve years old, and the tallest of all the children, but she looked no more than ten. Justine stopped several yards from the tree and watched Spence until she attracted his attention. He looked at her in surprise. She was making eyes at him.

Her father jumped up, looking frantically for a stick or switch, but before he could find anything, she ran behind the house out of sight. Floyd picked up a handful of sand and threw it at the children behind the tree. They dashed across the yard to the house.

"What you going to do about that, Floyd?" Spence asked, turning and looking at the corner of the house. He could see a portion of Justine's head as she watched him. "That looks real bad to me."

Floyd sat down, kicking at the bare ground with the heel of his shoe. He gazed at the earth dejectedly.

"Only God Himself knows," he said after a while.

Floyd had been having trouble with Justine all that summer. She had been running away from home and begging on the streets. He could not watch her every minute, because he had to stay at home and attend to his soft-drink and tobacco stand. He had built a little shed in front of his house near the street. It was just high enough for him to stand up in and wide enough to hold a few shelves for his stock of tobacco, candy, and soft drinks. He did not make much money, but the few dollars a week he earned did keep his family from starving.

He had tried to stay out of trouble himself, and he had succeeded so far. But Justine's behavior made him wonder how much longer he would be able to remain law-abiding. Other men in Poor Boy were selling marijuana in order to make a living for their families, and several of the women operated houses where men were dated.

He knew if he did not get his family away from Poor Boy, or provide them with a decent living, every one of his girls would grow up the way Justine had. He had already caught her in Mattie Watson's house, which was only a block away, where she was smoking a marijuana cigarette with one of Mattie's girls. Floyd had given her a hard whipping when he got her home, but he knew it would do no good. She had already found out, by that time, how to get money from men.

A small girl ran down the street and climbed up on the railing in front of Floyd's little store. He got up and went inside to wait on her.

"My mamma wants a big dime's worth of candy," she told Floyd. "She says give her the biggest dime's worth you've got, Mr. Sharp."

Floyd put some gumdrops into a paper sack and gave them to her. She dropped the dime into his hand and ran back home as fast as she could. Several of Floyd's little girls ran from the house hoping to get a piece of candy, but Floyd waved them away and locked the door.

Spence felt a hand pulling at his arm and he looked around to see Justine standing beside him.

"If I go up to your house, will you give me a quarter, Mr. Douthit?" she asked in a hushed hurried voice, watching her father coming back from the store. "Will you, Mr. Douthit?"

"You go on away," he said nervously, pushing her.

"I'll do anything, Mr. Douthit," she pleaded. "Honest, I will!"

She began backing away as her father came towards

54

the tree. Before turning and running, she smiled at Spence and blinked her eyes childishly.

Floyd picked up a handful of sand and threw it at her. Spence felt embarrassed.

"What did she say to you, Spence?" he asked worriedly.

Spence shook his head. He could not make himself tell the truth about the child.

"Nothing, Floyd," he lied. He began fanning his face and looking out over the canal. Floyd glared at him sternly. "But I reckon if I was you, I'd do my best to make her toe the mark. A young girl like that can get into a heap of trouble. I know all about it, because Mavis is out running wild right this minute."

"I'm in the midst of the worst muddle a man can get," Floyd said. His voice was husky and uneven. "It might not be so bad if there was only one, but I've got eight now and another one coming along. I'm liable to have ten or twelve before I quit." He shook his head despondently. "It's this God damn place that's doing it. It's Poor Boy. And it looks like God's paying me back for ever coming here to live and encouraging other folks to move in. If I hadn't come here and built that shack, there wouldn't be no Poor Boy, because I was the one who went and named it that, too. All that's against me, Spence. God's paying me back for sure."

"You can't do nothing about that now, Floyd," Spence said sympathetically. "Poor Boy's name's going to stick as long as people live in this part of the world."

"I could do something," Floyd insisted. "I could burn

55

the place down. Or I could make the city condemn it. Or something."

"The best thing you could do is go back home, Floyd. That'll get you out of this jam. I'm trying my best every day to get back to Beaseley County." He took out the road map and handed it to Floyd. "You wasn't figuring on slipping away without letting me know about it, was you? One of your little girls said you wanted to borrow my map."

"No," he answered reassuringly. "I just get homesick once in a while, and looking at the road back helps out a lot. If I could figure out a way to get back, I'd sure God do it, though. Jesus Christ, Spence, I've been away so long now that I'm getting to feel like I don't even belong back there. That sure is the worst kind of feeling to have, Spence. Jesus Christ, if it aint!"

A tall girl of about fifteen years came along the street, walking in the direction of town. When she was in front of the house, she smiled at Spence and Floyd and walked more slowly. She was better dressed than most girls in Poor Boy, and she was wearing high-heeled slippers. She was walking so slowly by that time that she was barely moving, and she was looking at them boldly and invitingly. When neither of them spoke to her, she went on down the street, watching them over her shoulder.

"That's Henry Dudley's daughter," Floyd said. "She's been going past here every afternoon about this time for the past month." They watched the girl go down the street until she was out of sight. "They can't even wait for dark to come no more," he said, shaking his head.

"They start for town in the middle of the afternoon so they'll be on hand when dark comes to get their share. Jesus Christ!"

Floyd's little girls ran across the yard. They both watched the children until they disappeared around the corner of the house. Spence got up and pulled his hat down hard over his head. The sun was getting low.

"One of these days I'm going to do something desperate, Spence," he said, looking up earnestly. "I don't know what, but something. Things can't go on like this. If I can't think of nothing better, I'm going to take these girls of mine over to the canal and drown the last one of them. The only reason I haven't already done it, I reckon, is because every time I think about it, it makes me feel sad. A man hates to lose everything he's got in the world, and those girls of mine are the only thing I've got to show for living, so far."

Spence took off his hat and sat down under the shade-tree again. He could not go away and leave Floyd feeling despondent.

CHAPTER FIVE

SPENCE SAT UNDER THE SHADETREE AN-
other hour. By that time Floyd was feeling better, and
so Spence put on his hat, telling Floyd not to do anything rash, and started home. He was half-way there when
he heard somebody walking behind him. He looked
around and saw Justine smiling at him. Without a word
he picked up a rock and threw it at her. She ran in the
direction of home as fast as she could.

When he turned the corner a few minutes later, he
looked down the street and saw a small black sedan in
front of his house. It did not look like any of the automobiles he could remember having seen before, and he
hastily stepped behind a tree. The rent collector had a
tan coupé, but he did not think the collector would
switch cars in an attempt to fool him, even though he
was nearly three months behind in rent. None of the
neighbors owned a car that was anywhere near as new
as it was, and he could think of no one he knew in the
South Side who still possessed any kind of car.

While he watched the house fifty yards away, a young woman walked out on the porch and looked up and down the street as though she were looking for some one. Spence ducked his head behind the tree and kept out of her sight. She looked a little like one of the schoolteachers who came to the house from time to time trying to find out why Mavis did not attend school; but the schools were closed in summer, and he decided it must be somebody else. By then he was curious to know who she was and what she wanted, and he knew he could not keep away from the house much longer. He walked slowly down the street, pretending to be looking straight ahead, but watching her all the time. As he reached the front yard, the young woman looked at him. Spence remembered that his water bill was past due, too, and he decided she might have been sent to collect for that. He turned into the yard and walked to the porch.

"Well, howdy, Miss," he said, taking off his hat.

"Are you Mr. Spencer Douthit?" she asked in a pleasant, businesslike manner. She appeared to be so friendly that he was surprised. She was not at all like the rent collector and others who tried to make him pay his debts. She was even smiling at him. "You are Mr. Douthit, aren't you?" she asked insistently.

"That's what they call me," he admitted reluctantly. He was still not able to decide whether to treat her like a friend or an enemy. "Did you come about the water bill, Miss?"

"No," she said with a quick smile. "Why did you ask?"

"Oh, I just happened to be thinking about it," he said, wondering what it could be that she wanted.

"Is your water bill past due?"

"A little, so I hear."

"That's too bad," she said, shaking her head as though it were her fault that it was unpaid. "I hope it's nothing that can't be easily taken care of."

"I don't let it worry me, it's the other folks who get upset. They act like the world's coming to an end if it aint paid in the next five minutes."

She sat down and opened a small briefcase. Spence walked up the steps to the porch and sat down on the edge of a chair where he could watch her. She was small and slender like Libby, and her dark brown hair was carefully combed. Her legs were long and shapely, and her knees, which were plainly visible under the hem of her skirt, were small and round. He could tell by her clothes that she came from some other section of the city, because she was much better dressed than any of the girls he had seen on the South Side. He guessed she was about twenty-one, possibly twenty-two.

"You know Mrs. Jouett, I believe," she said with a quick upward movement of her head. "Mrs. Jouett asked me to——"

"Why, that's the woman who came prowling around here yesterday!" Spence said at once. "I remember her! And to tell the truth, Miss, I never saw such a sorry excuse for a female before in my life. If I had to take my choice between rubbing up against her and a crabapple tree, I'd take the crabapple tree every time. Now, she's

61

nothing at all like you, Miss. You'd be a treat for any man."

She blushed and looked down at her hands. Spence could see her biting her lips to hide a smile.

"I am Miss Saunders," she spoke up abruptly, trying to make her voice sound harsh, "of the Welfare Department." She laid the briefcase on the floor and crossed her legs. "I was instructed to call on you, Mr. Douthit."

Spence opened his mouth to ask her why she had been told to call on him, but instead of saying anything he continued staring at her knees. Miss Saunders raised herself for a moment and tried to pull her skirt farther down. After several tugs at the hem she gave up and uncrossed her legs.

"I came to see you about your daughter, Mavis," Miss Saunders said, pausing for a moment. "Mavis is your daughter, isn't she, Mr. Douthit?"

"That's what I've always figured," he replied, staring at her.

"Well, then, I'd like to ask you some questions about her, Mr. Douthit. You must feel free to talk to me, because I am here to help you. You must not consider me a stranger trying to pry into your private affairs, but a sincere and trustworthy friend who wants to help your family adjust itself to the complex pattern of modern life. During cycles of economic and social readjustment, each member of the family unit must cooperate as to—well, as to unity. Is that clear, Mr. Douthit?"

"I can't say it is, Miss." He shook his head slowly from

62

side to side. "I don't seem to catch on to what you're driving at."

"Let me put it another way, Mr. Douthit. There are times when every family finds itself face to face with problems arising from maladjustment to reality, which is caused by the complex pattern of modern life. Now, some families achieve harmony by means of what you might call a family pow-wow, which of course is the ideal method. Others, like yourself for instance, accept advice from the Welfare Department. Now, I'm here to offer that assistance. All we ask is that you cooperate with us as to—well, as to that."

"Well," Spence said, "it just happens that that's the kind of fellow I am. I like to take an interest in everything that comes along." He watched her uncertainly, still wondering what she was talking about. "Maybe if you was to let me in on what's up I could help out, Miss."

"Good, Mr. Douthit!" she said enthusiastically. "I knew you would want to cooperate. Now, Mavis has been away from home for several days, hasn't she?"

"Three or four, I reckon."

"Have you made an effort to find her and bring her back home?"

"I couldn't do that, Miss, because I don't know where to look for her in this big city. If I could track her down, though, I'd sure go get her. Me and her Ma——"

Miss Saunders leaned forward, lowering her voice.

"I tried to speak to your wife while I was waiting for

you to come home, Mr. Douthit. She doesn't seem to be at all well today. Is she upset about Mavis?"

"Maud's been a little under the weather since she took too much tonic last night. Just don't pay her no mind, Miss, if she acts queer. It'll wear off in time. It always does."

"Well, getting back to Mavis—" she began.

"Let me tell you something, Miss," he interrupted. "All the blame for what Mavis' done ought to be put on Chet Mitchell, over there next door. It's his fault, pure and simple. If it hadn't been for Chet, Mavis wouldn't have run off like she done in the first place. I've been keeping my eye on him all summer, and I could tell he was waiting for a chance to get Mavis over there in his house. Then a few days ago while I was over in the South Side he done it."

"What did he do, Mr. Douthit?"

Spence hesitated for several moments. He thought she knew what he was talking about, and he looked at her strangely. She smiled encouragingly.

"Chet Mitchell adapted her, that's what," he said angrily. "He got her inside his house over there while his wife was down at the store and I was over in town and adapted her just like—well, just like you'd adapt any young girl who'd give you the chance."

"Why didn't you stop him, Mr. Douthit?" she asked stiffly.

"Stop him! How can you stop it when it's done done! She came prancing back over here, saying she was going off where she could have a good time with men all the time. Then off she went. But I'm going to get even with Chet Mitchell yet. You just wait and see if I don't!"

Miss Saunders looked down at the papers in her lap. She turned them over one at a time while she bit her lips thoughtfully.

"Mr. Douthit," she said, looking him straight in the eyes, "I would like to talk very frankly with you."

"Go right ahead, Miss," he urged, nodding. "You don't have to watch your language around me. I'm used to what talk you might've heard, and maybe some you aint heard yet. Anybody who's lived around Maud as long as I have——"

"I didn't mean that, exactly," she hastened to tell him. "What I mean is, I want to talk frankly with you about your daughter."

"I reckon I could listen to anything you could say," Spence said, watching her as she recrossed her legs.

"Mavis is on the verge of getting into serious trouble, Mr. Douthit." She looked directly into his face in an effort to gain his attention. "The only reason we have not yet taken direct action in the matter is because the Welfare Department always offers parents one final opportunity to exercise control over their children. That's why Mrs. Jouett came here to see you yesterday, and that's why I'm here now. The police made a report to us about Mavis, and we immediately took steps to find a way to return her to your care. If you will keep Mavis at home, supervising her life twenty-four hours a day, and prevent her from returning to the life she's now living, our department will recommend that she be placed in the custody of her parents. Mavis is thirteen and, consequently, a juvenile. If we are forced to turn the matter over to the police, they will take her to the juvenile court for a hearing. That means she will undoubtedly be committed to the Home For Wayward Girls. All this can be avoided, Mr. Douthit, if you will act on my advice. Is that clear now?"

"You mean Mavis is really cutting up that bad, Miss?"

"That's putting it very mildly, Mr. Douthit," she said severely. "She's living the life of a prostitute."

"And it took her only three or four days to get around to that?"

"Evidently."

"Well, that goes to prove she takes after her daddy, all right," he said, jerking his head emphatically. "That makes her my daughter, if anything does. When I set out to do something, I go whole-hog or nothing."

Miss Saunders was silent, and Spence did not know what to say after that. He knew she was waiting for him to answer, but the longer he waited, the more confused he became. When Mavis ran away, he was certain she would get into some kind of trouble, but he had never imagined it would result in bringing women like Mrs. Jouett and Miss Saunders to his house. He had always thought that when the police arrested a girl or woman, they merely sent her to the workhouse for thirty days and let it go at that.

"Are you sure you understand the seriousness of the situation, Mr. Douthit?" she prompted. "Did I make everything clear?"

Spence nodded, taking his time to answer. He was beginning to feel that he was more to blame for what had happened than Chet Mitchell was.

"If I could only get my family back to Beaseley County, there wouldn't be none of this trouble," he said regretfully. "My oldest daughter, Libby, is leaving and going back up there, and the rest of us'll be stranded down here for all time. I don't reckon it'd be fair to stop her, because she's got her heart set on marrying Jim Howard Vance. But, just the same, it's going to leave me and her ma, and Mavis, in a bad fix."

"I think I know how you feel, Mr. Douthit," she said as she leaned forward sympathetically. "You're not the only man with a family who wants to leave but can't raise the necessary funds. It's a very common occurrence these days. In spite of the fact that certain types of work may be plentiful, there are many men who are just not physically able to perform hard and strenuous labor. It would be different if you were skilled in some trade, because skilled labor is in demand, but I'm afraid the time has passed when a man your age can learn a new trade. We have hundreds of families on our lists that have been unable to make the social and economic adjustments which have become so necessary in modern life. Besides, men who are accustomed to rural surroundings sometimes never succeed in adjusting themselves to urban existence. There is often in the minds of such men a psychological resentment against crowded living conditions in a city, and homesickness and hunger for familiar scenes prevent ultimate adjustment. We who have made a study of such

67

things recognize this complex pattern in modern life. Now, until all of you can return to your former homes, the best we can do is to try to save the children, especially the young girls. I want you to know that I am really sorry, and I want to do everything I possibly can to help you."

"It aint my fault, Miss," he said. "I just can't seem to make a living down here no more like I did when the powder plant was running, and young girls like Mavis just aint going to be satisfied to sit still after they find out they can get money on the streets for new clothes and such knick-knacks as young girls like. I've tried and tried to think of some way to leave here before Mavis went wild, like she was bound to do, but time just caught up with me, and now it's done gone and happened. If it wasn't for Poor Boy, though, it wouldn't have happened as soon as it did. I blame it all on Poor Boy. It's nothing but a deep dirty hole for poor people like us, and it gets dirtier and deeper all the time. But, there has to be Poor Boys in the world, I reckon, or people like me couldn't find a place to live."

"One of these days we'll eliminate such conditions completely, Mr. Douthit. I agree with you that Poor Boy is a disgrace. Most of the crime in the city is bred right here. If I had my way, I'd burn every stick to the ground."

"Don't do that yet, Miss," he said with a startled look. "If you burned the houses and shacks down, we wouldn't have no place to go. We'd be worse off than before."

"I meant at the proper time, of course," she said. "Then

68

we'd erect a model housing settlement, with parks and playgrounds. It'd be a garden city."

"That wouldn't help me none if you charged rent, Miss. Folks like Floyd Sharp and me couldn't stay. We'd have to go off and hunt up another Poor Boy Town somewhere else."

Maud had come to the door and was looking at Miss Saunders. Spence glanced up at her.

"Who's that?" Maud asked sourly

"Why, that's the lady who's come to help us out," he said quickly. "She's going to help get Mavis back home."

"Why's she want to do that?"

"I don't know why, except that she makes a business of helping out folks like us."

"She looks to me like one of them women necktie sellers."

Miss Saunders got up and crossed the porch to where Maud was standing in the doorway. She smiled friendlily at Maud and held out her hand. Maud ignored it.

"I'm Miss Saunders," she said uncomfortably. "I've just been talking to your husband, Mrs. Douthit."

"I'll do all the talking to him that needs done," Maud said meanly, stepping backward and looking Miss Saunders up and down with a critical suspicious glance. Miss Saunders hastily adjusted her jacket. "I don't appreciate no women necktie sellers coming around here and trying to sport him behind my back," Maud said, raising her voice.

"But you don't understand, Mrs. Douthit," Miss Saunders protested. "I'm here in the official capacity as a repre-

69

sentative of the Welfare Department. We want to help your family adjust itself to the complex pattern of modern life."

Maud gazed at her stonily.

"Maud," Spence spoke up, "there aint a thing to get upset about. This lady don't do what you think she does——"

"I'll do my own thinking," she broke in, her voice sharp and commanding. She turned and glared at Miss Saunders. "Now, get going, sister, while you're able!"

Miss Saunders hastily gathered up her papers and briefcase. She retreated to the steps.

"Mrs. Douthit, it's only fair that you allow me to explain why I am here," she said.

"You heard me the first time, sister!"

Miss Saunders stopped when she reached the steps.

"I have a sacred duty to perform," she said, looking straight at Maud. "Mrs. Jouett has assigned me the task of adjusting your lives to the complex pattern of modern life. Nothing you can say will keep me from performing my duty, Mrs. Douthit. Nothing!"

"You'd better start performing that slinky behind of yours down the street!" Maud shouted.

Miss Saunders looked around wildly and jumped from the porch to the yard. Pausing, she glanced appealingly at Spence, who was backing away from the porch.

"I don't allow no women coming around here trying to get sported," Maud said evenly.

"Now, Maud, you oughtn't fly off the handle like that," Spence spoke up. "This lady here knows about a way to help us out. She aint prowling around for what you think she is." Spence turned to Miss Saunders. "Aint I right, Miss?"

"Yes," she said, swallowing hard. "That's right."

Maud came to the edge of the porch.

"You open that sassy mouth of yours again, babe, and I'll slap those fluffy tits of yours to hell and gone!"

Maud glared threateningly, and Miss Saunders clutched her briefcase tightly under her arm. Her hands were trembling so violently she lost all control over their movements.

"And you aint deaf, neither!" Maud said. "You heard me!"

Spence continued to move backward towards the street as he saw Maud come part way down the steps.

"I'm good and tired of catching you sporting women around here," Maud shouted at Miss Saunders. Miss Saunders turned and ran down the path. "That's right! You'd better run! If I ever got my hands on you, you'd never do no more sporting!"

Maud waited until Miss Saunders reached the street, and then, spitting disgustedly, she turned and went back into the house.

Spence saw Miss Saunders hastily getting into her car, and he raced across the yard to her.

"Miss, don't pay no mind to Maud," he pleaded urgently. "She always does a lot of big talking, but it aint nothing to worry about. It's just her way of speaking her mind."

71

Miss Saunders was not looking at Spence; she was keeping her eyes on the front door. Spence stuck his head through the car window and gripped the steeringwheel in order to prevent her from driving away.

"Now, about Mavis," he said nervously.

"This is awful," she said, glancing at Spence. Her face was pale with fright. "I've never been so mortified in my life. When I took my training in social welfare, nothing like this was ever mentioned. I never dreamed welfare work would bring me into contact with people like her. I'm afraid I've chosen the wrong type of work—I'd never, *never*, become used to that kind of language, Mr. Douthit! Oh, what will I do! What will I do! I'm so upset! No one ever talked to me like she did in all my life!"

"Don't quit, Miss, before you go ahead and help us out like you said you would," Spence pleaded. "I've been counting on that ever since you showed up this while ago. Please don't quit, Miss! It wouldn't be fair after getting my hopes up so high!"

"If I thought your wife was an exception——"

"Maud's the best exception that ever came down the big road, Miss! Just don't worry. Besides, you won't run up against many others in the world like Maud. She always was different from most women."

Miss Saunders bit her lips as though she realized she had to come to a decision. Spence watched her eagerly.

"Well," she said, sighing deeply, "will you promise to talk to Mavis, Mr. Douthit? And try to make her stay at home in your care?"

"I'll sure do the best I can, Miss," he said solemnly.

72

"All right, then," she said. She tore a slip of paper from her notebook and scribbled several words on it. "Now, this is where you can find her. Take the bus to the city limits, get off where it turns around, and walk down the highway about a hundred yards. You'll see the sign on the entrance."

Spence studied the slip of paper closely, spelling out the words.

"Why, I've heard of The White Turkey!" he exclaimed with surprise. "Is that where Mavis' at, sure enough?"

Miss Saunders nodded and started the motor.

"Well, dogbite my pecker!" he said. "I've heard a lot about that place, but I never thought I'd be going out there! They tell me it's a real high-class place."

"Don't forget what your purpose is when you get there, Mr. Douthit. I expect you to bring Mavis home with you. Do you understand perfectly?"

"Couldn't nothing go wrong, Miss," he assured her, releasing his grip on the steeringwheel. "Don't you worry."

"I'll have to come back in order to complete my report," she said, sighing. She glanced at the house. "But when I do come back, I want you to meet me out here in the street, Mr. Douthit. I don't think it would be wise to go any closer. Your wife is evidently upset."

"Maud'll be over her streak by the time you come back," he told her. "It comes and goes all the time like that."

73

"I certainly hope she'll be over it," she said as her car began moving. "Good-bye, Mr. Douthit!"

He watched the automobile disappear around the corner before looking down at the slip of paper in his hand and spelling out the words again.

CHAPTER SIX

FOR A LONG TIME AFTER MISS SAUNDERS
had left, Spence sat on the porch thinking about everything she had said, and wondering why a person like her,
who had never seen him before in her life, took so much
interest in his troubles and offered to help him, while at
the same time the world was so full of people, like the
storekeepers and rent collectors, who would not even
take the time to listen to him tell about them. Aside from
Floyd Sharp, who would have given Spence his last dime
if he thought Spence needed it more than he did, no one
had ever sympathized with him before, much less offered
any kind of help. Mrs. Jouett was a hard-hearted busy-
body; Miss Saunders was kind and understanding.

When he had first moved there, he found an open door
everywhere he went. Storekeepers waved to him as he
walked along the streets, even offering of their own accord to let him have anything he wanted on credit. The
rent collectors never pushed him when he was a month

or two behind, and even went so far as to tell him there was no hurry about the payments. He even bought a second-hand car from a dealer who asked for no more security than his and Maud's signatures scrawled on a piece of paper. All that had happened, of course, because he was working at the powder plant and drawing down sixty-two dollars and fifty cents every Tuesday. That was when Spence thought there were no finer people on earth than the citizens of the South Side. Then the powder plant closed down and he was out of work and everybody's attitude seemed to change over-night. His car, as well as most of his furniture, was attached; the rent collectors came around every few days threatening him with eviction; and, when he and his family began going hungry, the storekeepers refused to let him have food on credit.

Ever since then things had been gradually growing worse. When he saw somebody on the street who once had been cordial and friendly, he knew what the person was thinking. He was wondering how much longer the city would have to put up with those thieving squatters and ragged rent-dodgers in Poor Boy. Spence did not have to be told that he was no longer wanted there; he could read the open antagonism on almost every face he saw. Once he had passed a group of businessmen talking in front of a drug store and overheard part of their conversation. "How much longer are we going to stand for those godawful bastards over there in Poor Boy?" one man asked. "I can't answer that," one of the others said, "but there's something I will tell you. If we don't get rid of the sons-of-bitches soon, I'm going over there some night and plant a charge of dynamite under every shack in the place. When that goes off, it'll drive what's left of the bastards out of town." None of the men had recognized Spence, and he lingered on the corner for several minutes listening. "The funny thing about it is that there used to be a lot of fine people living over there before the riff-raff moved in and named it Poor Boy," another man had said. "The difference was that they were our own poor people, and not those down-and-outers from the hill country." Spence had walked away wondering what those same men would do if they lost their jobs and all their possessions and had to move to Poor Boy. It made him feel a lot better merely to think it could happen; for, after all, he had Beaseley County to go back to.

It was after sunset when Spence got up from his chair on the porch and went inside. The day's heat still clung to the walls and ceilings of the house, but already the evening breeze from the Gulf was blowing through the open doors and windows. Maud, wide awake, was sitting up on her cot and leaning her head and shoulders against the wall. She watched him walk through the room several times. Finally, he sat down on the chair beside her.

"I'm going after Mavis," he told her. He paused and waited for her to make some comment. Maud gazed at him indifferently. "I figure on finding her and bringing her straight back home, Maud. Of course, it may take time to locate her, but I'll bring her back for sure before I quit."

Maud still said nothing. Spence was hoping that the

77

prospect of returning Mavis home would put Maud into a more receptive mood for the suggestion he was going to make. He knew Maud had money, because he was positive Libby had left some under her pillow that morning, but he knew, too, that she suspected him of trying to get a good portion of it for himself. She eyed him coldly.

"It's going to be pretty nice having Mavis back home again," he said as though talking to himself. "She's going to be all tired out and glad to see you this time. A girl like Mavis would miss her ma a lot more than some others. She's still a baby in a lot of ways. Aint she, Maud?"

Maud continued to gaze at him suspiciously.

"It's a long way on the bus to where she's at, and I've got to be starting soon before it gets much later. She'll probably be hungry when I get there, and I ought to be in a position to get her something to eat. I wouldn't want her to come back hungry. Would you, Maud?"

Spence looked up at Maud with a quick motion of his head, but when his eyes met her steady unrelenting stare, he could detect no encouragement in her expression. He thought of the many times in the past when he had attempted to persuade Maud to let him have some of the money Libby had left for her, but none of the arguments he had previously used seemed then to be appropriate. He sat thinking about it for a long time, trying his best to bring to mind something that would touch Maud's stony heart. Slowly a smile spread over his face.

"You know, Maud," he said unhurriedly. "I've been thinking a lot since Mavis went away, and dogbite it if

78

I don't believe I'm dead right. I don't think it would've ever come over me if it hadn't been for what happened right here yesterday afternoon."

He paused significantly and looked at Maud, nodding to himself with conviction. Maud was unable to hide her curiosity.

"What you talking about, Spence?"

"The more I think it over, the righter it seems."

"What does, Spence?"

"And it wouldn't be at all hard to do, neither."

Maud reached over and grasped his arm. She shook him determinedly.

"Aint you going to tell me, Spence?" she begged.

Spence glanced at her briefly and got to his feet.

"Dogbite it, why didn't I think about that before?" he said to himself. He slapped his thigh roughly.

"Is it about Mavis, Spence?"

He walked up and down the room several times, finally coming back to the cot and looking down at Maud thoughtfully. He nodded his head as if only then had he found time to answer her question.

"What about her, Spence?"

"We'll get Mavis married to somebody, like Libby's marrying Jim Howard," he told her as he sat down beside her. "But this time we'll find somebody who's got a little money, or else a good-paying job. Then as soon as she's married, we'll let him furnish the money for us to go back home. It won't be hard to do at all, because there's plenty of men who could be pushed into marrying Mavis. She's young enough to suit the most particu-

79

lar, and being away like she has, she'll have picked up a lot of tricks she ought to know. It looks now like it was a good thing what Chet Mitchell done to her, after all, because if he hadn't, Mavis wouldn't have got it into her head to run off, and then I'd never have thought of it. But, just the same, it aint going to stop me from getting even with him, because it's the right thing to do."

When he stopped to get his breath and to see what effect he had had on Maud, he could tell instantly that she was thinking about the proposal. She was no longer staring glassy-eyed at him, as if to say that she would never be tricked by anything he could think up; but, instead, she appeared to be thinking seriously about it. As he watched her, he realized that he, too, was taking it seriously, and the longer he sat there, the more firmly convinced he became that something could be done.

"You know anybody who'd marry her?" Maud asked.

"No, not off-hand I don't, but with all the men there are around, there's bound to be one who'd do it in a jiffy," he said excitedly. "Couldn't all of them hold out against her, especially anybody wanting to marry one as young as Mavis. They just don't come much younger than she is, anyhow. It ought to be real easy."

"How'd we be sure he had some money?"

"I'd see to that before I'd let her start prissing around. Besides, I'd warn her that loving up a rich man aint a bit different than loving up a poor one, except that the rich man would expect more for his money. Anyway, it's just as easy for a woman to have something to show for all the handling she does, as it is to end up with nothing."

"It's a pity I didn't know about that twenty-five years ago," Maud said bitterly. "Instead of being where I am right this minute, I'd be living on easy street."

Spence got up and found a shirt that was cleaner than the one he was wearing. After he had made the exchange, he wet his hair with water and slicked it down with Maud's brush.

"You can let me have a little of that money now, Maud," he said with assurance. "I'll need it if I'm going to make a good start."

He came to the cot and held out his hand.

"If you spend all my money, and I find out this aint nothing but a trick, you'll never get another penny from me as long as I live," she warned him. "Now, I mean exactly what I say, Spence Douthit!"

"Oh, that aint nothing to worry about, Maud," he said, thrusting his open palm at her and waiting. "I've done made up my mind about marrying Mavis off. It's going to get us back home to Beaseley County."

Maud put her hand under the pillow and drew out five dollars. She looked at it as if silently debating whether or not she was doing the wise thing.

Spence took it from her before she could change her mind and put it carefully into the watch-pocket of his trousers.

"Now, you just lay there and don't worry none, Maud," he said soothingly. "This's going to turn out just the way it sounded when I mentioned it. I'll be back here with Mavis before you know it."

Without wasting any more time, he got his hat and

81

left the house. All the way down the street to the bus stop he thought about the possibility of finding somebody to marry Mavis, and by the time he got to the bus line he was satisfied in his own mind that it could be accomplished.

It was a long ride across the city, and he had to change busses twice on the way, once on the South Side, and again at the main terminal. Getting on the right busses and arguing with the drivers over the transfers had worn him out, and by the time he reached the end of the bus line at the city limits, he felt as if he had done a day's work.

All the other passengers got up and hurried off into the night as soon as the bus stopped. Most of them were clerks and office workers who were in a hurry to get home for supper, and Spence, unaccustomed to the pushing and shoving, waited until they all got off before going to the door. When he got there, the driver was counting fares and writing figures in a small red book.

Spence nudged him with his elbow.

"That's the place down the road yonder, aint it, son?" he asked. "Aint that The White Turkey?"

The driver put away his fare-book and looked up. He was a young man of about twenty-three or twenty-four with a small brown mustache. He took out a cigarette and lit it.

"It sure is, mac," he said, nodding and blowing out smoke. "Your first trip, huh?"

"It's the first time I ever got anywhere near it," Spence said. "I wouldn't be coming out here now if Miss Saunders hadn't put me up to it. I've been hearing about The White Turkey for a long time, but I never figured I'd be coming out here."

"Who's she, mac? One of the girls?"

"Who, Miss Saunders? Not exactly, I don't think. But she talks like she knows a lot about it."

The bus driver sucked on the cigarette several times in quick succession, filling the air with smoke. Spence started down the steps to the street.

"Well, take it easy, mac," he warned Spence. "Don't let the girls burn you."

Spence turned around and looked up at the boy through the open door. He chuckled, shaking his head.

"I don't have to worry, son," he said. "My daughter works out here at The White Turkey."

The driver opened his mouth as if to speak, but several moments passed before he said anything.

"Well, I'll be God damned!" he exclaimed, looking closely at Spence. "Maybe you're right, and I'm wrong, mac!"

Spence was about to start walking down the highway when he remembered what he planned to do. He came back and leaned inside the door.

"You make a pretty good wage driving a bus, don't you, son?" he asked.

"Fair," the boy replied. "Could be worse."

"How'd you like to get yourself married?"

"Some day, mac. There's no hurry. I'm having a pretty good time as it is."

83

"You wouldn't want to marry a good-looking girl who'd treat you first rate, and do it right away?"

The driver pulled on the cigarette several times and flipped the butt through the door over Spence's head.

"What's the catch, mac?" he asked.

"There ain't no catch, son," Spence said hopefully. "If you wanted to do it, I can fix it up in no time. Just say the word, and I'll get busy."

"You must have something that's too hot to handle yourself."

"I'm only trying to do you a favor, son."

"Say! You've got screws loose in your head, mac," he laughed. "What are you trying to do, sell me a mail-order bride?"

"It's Mavis—my daughter," Spence said quickly.

"The one who you said works at The White Turkey?"

"Sure, that's her! Now, how about it, son?"

The boy raced the motor and engaged the gears. The bus began moving slowly away.

"Mac, you sure are nuts if you think I'd marry one of those daisies!" he shouted through the door. "I'll take my beating some other way!"

Spence watched the bus turn around and roar down the road in the direction of town. When its red and green tail lights disappeared in the night, he started walking towards the small electric sign a hundred yards away. As he got nearer the long low building, he could see fifteen or twenty automobiles parked on each side of it. Several men got out of a car and went inside.

He went up to the entrance and pushed open the door. A bright spotlight, shining directly in his face, blinded him momentarily. Shielding his eyes with both hands, he moved past the door into a narrow hall. Somebody stepped out of the darkness and grabbed his arm. Spence could see a hard tight-lipped face staring at him, and then a second face, dark and scarred, appeared before him.

"What's your name?" one of the men asked gruffly.

"Why, I'm Spence Douthit."

"Where're you from?"

"Why, I live down on the South Side."

"What do you do for a living?"

"I used to work at the powder plant before it closed down," Spence said.

One of the men shoved him back into the spotlight.

"This is a private club for members only," the man with the scarred face said.

"Oh, that's all right," Spence spoke up. "I go to Bill Tarrant's down on the South Side every now and then. It's a private club, too."

"Search him, Jake," the scar-faced man said. "Got a pistol or knife on you?" he asked Spence.

"I sure aint," Spence said.

He felt hands patting him under the arms, around his hips, and all the way down both legs.

"He's clean," the tight-lipped man said.

"Okay, bud," the other one said to Spence, giving him a shove. "Go on in."

Spence stumbled through the door and stepped into a large room filled with the odor of tobacco smoke, beer,

85

and sweaty bodies. Loud, ear-throbbing music was coming from a juke box that blazed with constantly-changing colored lights. He pushed through the crowd of men towards the bar on the opposite side of the room. Most of the men were wearing short-sleeved open-necked sportshirts, although a few of them had on expensive, light-weight, summer suits. It looked to Spence as if there were at least seventy or eighty men in the room, and he was amazed to see such a large crowd. There were rarely ever more than thirty or forty men at Bill Tarrant's at one time.

He was still trying to make his way through the crowd to the bar when he felt somebody pressing against him. When he looked to see who it was, he was surprised to see a young girl smiling up at him. Spence judged her to be fifteen or sixteen, although the manner in which she had piled her hair on top of her head made her look several years older. Spence stepped back as she continued pressing her body against his. He had never in his life seen a girl wear so few clothes in public, and those so misplaced. Her dress did not really begin until it started at her waist, and then it went all the way down to the floor, but even that was split down the front. A wisp of lace was thrown over her shoulder as if she did not know what else to do with it, but he considered it a complete waste for all the good it did. He stared open-mouthed at her naked body. Down in Poor Boy, on hot midsummer afternoons when the temperature got up into the hundreds, Maud and Myrt, Libby and Mavis, like most of the other girls and women, thought nothing of going

86

about the house naked, because it was tne only way to keep their clothes from becoming damp with perspiration, but none of them had ever gone into the street or to public places without putting on most of their clothes.

"Lonesome, big boy?" the girl asked, putting her hand on his shoulder and leaning against him while her eyelashes fluttered tantalizingly.

"Well now, I don't know about that," he said uneasily as he gazed at her. "When I came in here just now, I didn't think about that at all."

"But you could be, couldn't you, big boy?" she said, pushing a knee against his leg.

"That aint far from the truth, anyhow."

"How'd you like to have a party with me? Huh?"

"Well, I hadn't thought much about it, but——"

He looked around uneasily. There were men standing only a few feet away, and he was surprised that they were not paying any attention to the girl.

"But, what?" she asked.

"Well, it's something it wouldn't be hard to think about," he said.

She slipped her arm through his and leaned against him intimately. Spence looked at her bosom.

"What's the matter, big boy?" she asked, shaking his arm.

"Miss, maybe it aint none of my business," he said, leaning close to her and lowering his voice so no one else would hear, "maybe it aint none of my business at all, but your tits are showing."

She stepped back, withdrawing her arm from his, and

stared at him queerly for a moment. Then she suddenly burst into loud laughter.

Spence felt embarrassed and uneasy. He was sure everybody in the room was laughing at him. He looked around hastily at the men nearby, who still were not even looking in his direction; and when he turned back to look at the girl, she had left. He saw her running to another girl who was standing near the door. Still laughing, she pointed at Spence. Spence turned and made his way through the crowd towards the other side of the room as quickly as he could. The juke box music started again, and he was glad he could no longer see the girls or hear their laughter. He found a place at the bar where he would be completely out of sight.

CHAPTER SEVEN

"You can give me a bourbon and a beer chaser," Spence told the large bald-headed man behind the bar. He spread a crumpled dollar bill on the damp wood and smoothed the wrinkles out of it with his fingers.

The bartender took a good look at Spence.

"Where you from, friend?" he asked. "I don't remember ever seeing you around here before."

"I live down on the South Side," Spence told him, pushing the dollar across the bar. "Better make that a double bourbon and a glass of beer."

"Maybe I won't be seeing you around again, either," the bartender said, nodding his head up and down. He set-up a bottle and a glass and drew the beer. Then he took Spence's dollar and rang it up on the cash register. "But if you're used to it, friend, it aint none of my business how you drink it. I'm paid to tend bar, not to give out advice."

He gave Spence a final emphatic nod and went up to the other end of the bar to wait on some of the other customers. Spence tossed off the bourbon and beer and quickly refilled the whiskey glass. In a few moments the bartender came back and put the bottle on the shelf.

"We always let a new customer do that just once," he said, eyeing Spence significantly. "The boss says it's good for business—just once!"

He leaned an elbow on the bar and watched Spence.

"Dogbite it if this aint the first time I ever saw so many young girls with only part of their clothes on," said Spence, waving his arm at the room behind him. "How in the world do you stand it, fellow?"

The bartender placed both arms on the bar and leaned forward. He was tapping Spence with a finger.

"Friend, you get used to it," he said. "It's like anything in life that you see enough of. After a while what you see around here is just like being a farmer and walking through your cornfield and shucking off an ear here and an ear there to find out how the crop's coming along. See what I mean, friend?"

He winked at Spence, jerking his head to one side with an emphatic nod. Spence took a drink of bourbon.

"It used to be," the bartender said, looking up and down the length of the bar and running his hand over his bald head, "that there were two kinds of women. Bad and good. Nowadays there's only one kind. Good-and-bad." He nodded his head with quick up and down motions. "See what I mean, friend?"

Before Spence had a chance to say anything, the bartender began tapping him in the arm.

"Parents don't seem to give a damn what becomes of their daughters any more," he was saying. "It looks to me like all they raise daughters for is to turn them into whores when they're big enough to be accommodating." He shook his head sadly. "It wasn't this way when I was growing up. In those days people took a lot of pride in their children, and the only women you'd find in a place like this would be those old tough-titted whores. Now, just look at those girls out there! They shouldn't be here. They ought to be at home. But, men with young daughters are out batting around with other men's young daughters every night, and they're so busy doing it, they don't give a good God damn what becomes of their own."

"I know what you mean," Spence, nodding in agreement, said, "because I've got two of my own. The youngest one's just turned thirteen, and I've been wracking my brain to find a way to get her—" He stopped and stared open-mouthed at the bald-headed bartender.

"What's wrong?" he asked Spence, turning around and glancing at himself in the mirror behind the bar. "Why you looking at me like that?"

"Say!" Spence exclaimed, putting down the empty bourbon glass. "How'd you like to get married? You've got a fine job here, and you look like——"

The bartender reached out a big heavy hand and slapped Spence on the shoulder.

"Friend," he said with a chuckle, "you're looking at a man who's tried it three times and learned his lesson the hard way. The last woman I married ran a beautyshop. Now, if you don't know what goes on in some of those places, I'm here to tell you. To start with, she had a little back room in her place. I didn't pay no more than ordinary attention to it the first time I saw it, but one day, after I'd been married about a week, I went in through the back door and caught her in there with two young girls who'd been coming there a couple times a week all summer. There aint no use in me telling you what went on in there, because if you live down on the South Side you know what goes on all around you as well as I could tell you. So, that's when I picked up my hat and scooted, and I've been scooting ever since as far as getting married these days is concerned. Yes, sir! I'm as cured as a smokehouse ham! No more marrying for me until times change!"

"That aint no reason to give up completely," Spence said doggedly. "Now, I've got a daughter who'd make a fine wife for a man. She aint old enough to be ruined, much. And she'd learn in no time how to take care of a man."

The bartender left to draw several beers for customers. He was away for several minutes.

"Friend," he said when he got back, "I appreciate everything you said, but I just aint a marrying man no more till times change. However, I may be able to help you out." He raised his head and looked around the room behind Spence.

"How's that?" Spence asked, wondering.

"There's a fellow who comes here every night who might be just the man you're looking for." He continued looking around the room. "Of course I can't say for sure. But if there's anybody who would be willing, it's Bubber."

He straightened up and walked to the other end of the bar. After he had looked at the other side of the room, Spence saw him beckoning to somebody. When he got back to Spence, a young man of about twenty-five, who looked dissipated and sallow, elbowed his way to the bar. He was dark-haired and well-dressed, but the first thing about him that Spence noticed was his grin. He grinned as if it were the only thing he had ever done in his whole life.

"Come here, Bubber," the bartender said, reaching over and pulling him to the bar. "I want you to meet a friend of mine." He nodded at Spence. "Bubber, meet—" The bartender looked at Spence. "Say, what's your name, anyway?"

"Why, I'm Spence Douthit."

"Sure. That's it. Bubber, meet Spence Douthit."

"Hi," Bubber said, still grinning broadly.

"Well, howdy," Spence said eagerly.

"Give us a new set-up, Mike," the boy told the bartender. He placed an elbow on the bar, leaned heavily upon it, and grinned at Spence. While the drinks were being poured, Bubber drew a five-dollar bill from his pocket and tossed it on the bar.

"Now, friend," the bartender said as he leaned forward, "here's somebody you ought to talk it over with. Bubber gets married every once in a while, just to keep in practice. He's in-between wives right now, and it's about time for him to try again. Aint that right, Bubber?"

Bubber grinned foolishly. "That's right, Mike," he said as he pushed his glass across the bar for a refill.

"What kind of work do you do?" Spence asked. "You've got a job, aint you?"

Mike, the bartender, chuckled.

"I'm in the commission business," Bubber replied with a spreading grin. "You know about that, don't you?"

"Can't say that I do," Spence admitted. "Does it pay you a good wage?"

"Does it pay good wages!" Bubber laughed. "I'll say!"

"You make plenty of money then?"

"Listen, fellow, you don't have to worry about me making money. I can always make plenty of dough."

Spence chewed the tip of his tongue nervously. He disliked the appearance of Bubber's pimply, spongy face and the constant foolish grin, but he could not ignore the fact that the boy might be persuaded to marry Mavis.

"Tell me about this girl," Bubber said. "What is she? Blonde or brunette?" Spence watched the boy's silly face and wondered why he grinned all the time. "If you know somebody I might want to marry, you ought to tell me what she looks like, fellow." He nudged Spence hard in the ribs. "That's important."

"Oh, she's good-looking, all right," Spence said quickly. "She's better-looking than most of the girls you see running around."

94

"That's good enough for me, to start with," Bubber nodded. "Just so she aint a blonde. She aint, is she? The last one I married was a blonde, and I'm off them for a while."

"She's got dark brown hair that's almost black at times," Spence said.

"How old?"

"Well, I couldn't say exactly, not off-hand," Spence replied uneasily. "How old would you want her to be, for example?"

"The younger the better. They don't come too young."

"And you might want to marry her, being that she's young, and all that?"

"Sure! Why not? Hell, I haven t been married in a long time! I'll take a chance, fellow!"

"And you won't back out at the last minute?"

"Not if she's got what it takes," he replied, shoving his grinning face close to Spence's and slapping him on the back. "That's what counts, isn't it, Mike?"

"It aint what takes," the bartender said knowingly. "It's what gives that counts."

Spence clutched Bubber's arm. "If I was to go get her and bring her here, would you make up your mind about marrying her, right away?" he asked eagerly.

"Pal, that wouldn't be hard to do if I liked her looks, would it?" Bubber said. "Where's she at now?"

"I'll get her!" said Spence, patting the boy's arm. "Just you don't go away!" He drank the remainder of the bourbon and beer, slapping Bubber on the back when he finished. "Aint no reason why you won't like her, son,"

95

he assured Bubber. "She keeps me pricked up around the house, and I'm a close relation."

He gave Bubber a friendly pat on the back and pushed his way from the bar. He went through the room looking at the girls. When he got to the other side, he stopped and looked around bewilderedly. He had seen five or six girls, but none of them was Mavis. While wondering how to go about finding her, he felt somebody pressing against him. He turned with a start and saw another girl in a topless gown smiling up at him. She was dressed almost exactly like the first girl he had talked to.

"Let's go somewhere and sit down, big boy," she suggested invitingly. "How'd you like that, big boy?"

"To tell God's own truth, Miss, I aint got the time right now," said Spence, trying to walk away from her.

"Aw, come on and loosen up," she said, pulling at his arm and squeezing his hand. "My name's Jerrie. I'll treat you right, big boy. You don't have to look any more. I know how to give you a good time."

Spence raised up on his toes and tried to see what had become of Bubber. Spence could not see him at the bar, and he became agitated with worry. He pushed at the girl to make her go away.

"Miss, I'm sorry about it, but I've just got to be going," he said nervously as he tried to make her leave. "As soon as I find Mavis, maybe I——"

"Mavis is out right now," Jerrie said promptly. She clung tenaciously to his arm. "Why don't you let me give you a good time, big boy? You don't have to wait for Mavis."

"Where's she at?" he asked, turning to her.

"She's out on a call."

"But she's the one I've got to see," Spence protested as he felt himself being pulled towards a door.

"That's what you think!" Jerrie said teasingly. "You just don't know Jerrie, big boy! I'll show you why you don't have to wait for her! Come on!"

She led him through a door and into a larger room. There were two large crap tables on one side of the room, another bar on the opposite side, and a small dance floor in the center. There were tables and chairs circling the dance floor, and a raised platform against the wall, where three Negro boys sat surrounded by a strange-looking assortment of musical instruments. One of the Negroes was playing the piano when Spence and Jerrie crossed the floor and sat down at an unoccupied table.

A waiter was standing at Spence's elbow almost immediately. Spence wondered how he had been able to appear at his side so quickly.

"What'll it be?" he asked gruffly.

"Bourbon and beer," Spence said without thought.

Jerrie nodded to the waiter and slid her chair close beside Spence. He felt her arm around his neck.

"What was all that talk you were trying to give me?" she asked, pouting a little. "Don't you like me, big boy?"

"It aint that, Miss," he protested. "I've hardly had time to make up my mind either way, even if I wanted to. But I've got to find Mavis so I can——"

"Look, big boy!" Jerrie said, locking her arm around his neck and pulling him to her. "Let's not get into an

97

argument about Mavis. We swap dates all the time. She won't be sore at you."

"This is different, Miss. I'm working on a sure-fire scheme that's going to——"

There was an ear-splitting noise as music blared from half a dozen musical instruments. The three Negro boys were playing the piano with their hands, blowing horns, and beating drums with their feet. Spence looked around just as the curtains parted over a door beside the platform and saw a girl come dancing across the floor. He sat up erectly in his chair. The girl was holding a small black fur muff in front of her.

The waiter placed the bourbon and beer on the table and nudged Spence in the ribs with the knuckle of his thumb.

"A dollar, pop," he said, holding the open palm of his hand under Spence's nose.

Spence reached into his pocket and took out a dollar.

The girl was whirling around in the center of the dance floor, holding the little black muff tight against her body. The music suddenly slowed down and she began moving her body backward and forward while her feet remained still. Spence rose up from his chair in order to see better, but Jerrie pulled him back.

"Now, look here!" he protested angrily. "That's something I know good and well I want to see!"

The dancer moved across the floor to one of the near-by tables and stood in front of it until one of the men tossed her a coin. She stooped down and picked it up, and then she held the muff behind her back for a moment.

98

Spence reached for the bourbon and drank it down in a gulp. Jerrie was tugging at his arm.

"Give her a quarter, big boy," she urged him. "Go on and be big-hearted."

Spence took out a quarter and held it up for the girl to see. She turned and danced towards Spence's table. He leaned forward and gave her the money, and she began swaying from side to side in time with the music. A man behind Spence was leaning on his shoulder and digging his elbow into the side of Spence's head.

"Throw it away, baby!" the man on Spence's shoulder shouted at the top of his voice.

Spence wanted to see the muff thrown away, too, but he could not endure the painful blows on his ear any longer. He stood up, drew back his fist, squinting one eye shut as he took careful aim, and hit the man on the jaw as hard as he could. The stranger staggered backward into the crowd.

The girl was weaving her hips in a circular motion when Spence sat down. He licked his parched lips and felt blindly for the beer chaser. The girl was slowly raising the fur muff over her head, and he raised the glass. Before he could drink the beer, he felt somebody leaning heavily on his shoulder. He took his eyes from the girl long enough to recognize the same man again.

"Shake that thing at me, baby!" the man shouted over the top of Spence's head.

She looked up and smiled. The muff was high over her head by then, but the stranger was pounding at Spence's ears with both fists. He was afraid he would miss some-

99

thing if he got up and slugged the stranger again, so he put his arms over his ears and watched the girl. She had turned around, and her hips were wiggling in time with the music.

"Now aint that something?" the man said, gripping Spence's head with both hands and jerking him roughly. Spence found himself staring the man in the eyes. "Pal, that is something, aint it?"

The music stopped and the girl ran across the floor. As she disappeared through the curtains, pennies, nickels and dimes showered around the platform, and the Negro boys jumped down and began sweeping up the coins with their hands.

The stranger who had been holding Spence's head in a vise-like grip, released it and walked away.

Spence wet his dry lips and looked at Jerrie beside him. She was smiling.

"That sure left me feeling like a rabbit with his balls caught in a sewingmachine," he said, wiping the perspiration from his forehead.

Jerrie snuggled against him.

"There'll be another show in five minutes," she said.

"You mean there'll be another girl coming out here just like that one did with only a little fur muff?" he asked unbelievingly.

"All the girls take turns." She nodded. "It's part of our job."

"You, too?"

"Of course."

"Well, dogbite it!" he said, shaking his head. "I sure

would like to know what they're going to think of next!"

The waiter was standing at Spence's side, jabbing his thumb-knuckle into his ribs.

"How much money you got left?" Jerrie asked.

Spence pulled out two one-dollar bills and a few nickels and dimes.

"Is that all?" Jerrie asked disgustedly.

Spence nodded.

"No more drinks," she said sharply to the waiter. He turned and walked away.

"You come with me," she said authoritatively. She got up and pulled Spence to his feet. "We're going to the boarding-house."

"Now, wait a minute, Miss!" he protested. "You said another girl was coming out here in five minutes, and I want to see more of that."

"The hell you do!" she said sternly, giving his arm a jerk. "You're coming with me before you spend what you've got left. Come on, big boy!"

"But I don't want to miss seeing a sight like that again," he told her, trying to pull his arm from her grip. "You aint being a bit fair, Miss!"

"To hell with that!" she said crossly as she pulled him away from the table and across the dance floor. "We're going to the boarding-house!"

She made him go through a door and down a long dimly-lit hall. When they reached the end of it, Spence saw a large Negro woman reading a love story magazine under a shaded floor lamp.

"Mamie," Jerrie said. still holding to Spence's arm, "what's vacant?"

The Negro woman, carefully marking a page, laid the magazine down and got to her feet.

"Howdy, Miss Jerrie," Mamie said pleasantly. "I aint hardly seen you all night before."

The Negress looked sharply at Spence, quickly sizing him up. After inspecting him from head to foot she tossed her head disdainfully and walked away. They followed her down the hall until she pushed open one of the doors and went inside to turn on the light. When she came out, she stood beside the door with her hands folded over her stomach. She waited expectantly until Spence walked past her into the room without giving her a quarter.

"Huh!" she said contemptuously. "Some more of that good-for-nothing white trash!"

She slammed the door shut.

When Spence looked around the room, he saw Jerrie standing in front of the mirror and combing her hair. He watched her, swaying on his feet. The bourbon-and-beer made it difficult for him to look at anything very long before tables, chairs, and walls began to float before his eyes. He reached out for the foot of the bed in order to steady himself.

"Where's Mavis?" he demanded in a loud voice. "I want to see Mavis!"

Jerrie shook him roughly.

"I told you once that Mavis is out on a call!" she said. "She might not come back at all tonight! Now, shut up like I tell you!"

"I've got to find Mavis, because he might not wait much longer," Spence said, turning and stumbling towards the door. "That's why I've got to go get her."

Jerrie beat him to the door.

"I aint going to lose him, no matter what happens!"

"Oh, shut up!" she cried impatiently.

She turned him around, and he kept on walking until he struck the side of the bed and fell across it.

"Where's the money?" she demanded.

Spence took out the two one-dollar bills. She snatched them from his hand and pinned the bills to her dress.

"I should have got you in here before you spent the rest on drinks," she said, coming back to the bed. She sat down beside him. "French or straight?" she asked coldly, shaking him until he opened his eyes.

"Huh?" Spence muttered.

"You heard me, you bastard!" she snapped, slapping his face until his eyes blinked with pain.

He raised himself on his elbow and rubbed his stinging cheeks. She knocked his hand aside and slapped him again as hard as she could.

"Dogbite my pecker if this aint a topsy-turvy world," he said, watching her with a puzzled expression. "First, I get glad-handed all over the place, then next thing I know I'm getting slapped like nobody's business. And if it hadn't been for Miss Saunders, I'd never known the first thing about it. Things sure work out in a queer way sometimes."

"What are you talking about, anyway?" she asked.

Spence was looking at her curiously.

"Why don't you answer me, you bastard!" she said in a loud voice. Before he could say anything, she began slapping him on the face again. He held his arms around his head until she stopped.

"Miss," He said, "I may be forgetful, but I know good and well I didn't bargain for nothing like this."

"You bastard, you!" she cried, striking his face as hard as she could.

CHAPTER EIGHT

MAUD, SITTING UP IN BED WITH HER BACK resting comfortably against the wall, had been talking endlessly for the past two hours. At a time like that talking seemed to be even less of an effort than breathing. She had already blamed him for everything under the sun he could have thought of if he had been doing the talking, besides a lot more he would never have thought of, and still she talked. Spence sat placidly in the next room with his feet on the kitchen table, a grim smile on his sun-creased face. After twenty-five years of marriage he had learned to sit still and keep his mouth shut when Maud got started on one of her talking streaks. The summer heat, which at that time of the year blanketed the earth from shortly after sunrise to sunset, brought beads of perspiration to his face. Every now and then he raised his arm cautiously and wiped his damp forehead with his shirtsleeve. The swarm of black, fat, lazy flies that were always in the house droned in never-ending circles around the stopper in the sorghum jug on the table.

"If you wasn't so durn lazy and worthless, you'd do something about getting me back home except talk," Maud said huskily, her throat beginning to feel sore after talking for most of the morning. "It's been a whole year now since you said we was going home, and we're still here, worse off than ever, and getting in a more sorry fix every time the sun rises. If I'd married me a hard-working man with some gristle, like some of the fine beaus I turned down to marry you, I wouldn't be in the sorry fix I'm in, and you know it. None of them wouldn't sit there like you do from one year to the next, and do nothing. You told me if I married you, you'd build me a fine white house with a cellar and attic, and now here I am down here in Poor Boy where even the niggers and Mexicans wouldn't live if they was paid for it. I was a durn fool to listen to you, Spence Douthit. You turned out to be so good-for-nothing even your own daughters won't stay in the same house with you. And I don't blame Libby and Mavis one bit for staying away, neither. No, I don't! If I was young like I once was, and good-looking like them, with a sporty figure that brings out the gristle, I'd get out and have myself a whopping good time, too. There's plenty of men who'd sport me, because I was never backward about fetching a man, even if I do say so myself. You just ask any of my old beaus if you don't believe me. But just look at me now! I aint got my looks left, not after wearing them out on you for twenty-five years, and I have to lay here in this bed from one day to the next, all helpless and puny, and couldn't sport a man if I could reach out and touch one right now. On top of all that, you go out somewhere last night and spend the five dollars I was fool enough to give you out of Libby's hard-earned wages—" she paused until she could get enough breath to finish, "—and still don't bring Mavis back with you after making up such a high-sounding lie about it."

Spence drew a deep breath and crossed his legs in a more comfortable position on the kitchen table. He knew it would be a waste of time and effort for him to attempt to get a word in until Maud was ready for him to say something. The swarm of flies buzzed protestingly when the movement of his feet disturbed their peaceful circling of the sorghum jug.

"Are you listening to me, Spence Douthit?" Maud called garrulously, raising her voice. "Are you still in the kitchen?"

"I'm right here listening, Maud," he said meekly.

There was a short interval of silence in the house before she began again. Spence closed his eyes momentarily, grateful for the few moments of peace.

"I don't know what you done last night, Spence Douthit, but I know it was something nasty. Whatever it was, it was a mean low-down nasty thing to do. If you done what I think, you got drunk on part of Libby's hard-earned wages, and then spent the rest getting it sported out of you. Ever since I've known you, Spence Douthit, you've been chasing after a smell-and-a-squeal like a good-for-nothing old hound dog who can't do nothing but sniff, noway. There was a time when you'd quit work spang in the middle of the day to go off looking for something to sport. You've been running around with your tail in the air ever since I first laid eyes on you, and I ought've had better sense than let you go off from here last night with Libby's five dollars in your pocket. I don't care how many wild schemes you'd thought up to get Mavis back here, I ought've had better sense than listen to you. But don't think you're the only one who could cut a shine, Spence Douthit! If I had my looks back, even a small part of them, I could go out and get sported, too. And don't think I wouldn't do it, neither! I'd hist my skirt and have the men poking hards at me all over this part of the world. There used to be a time twenty-some odd years ago, just before I was fool enough to marry you, when real men with plenty of gristle would come from all over on Sunday afternoons just to look at me and speculate. There wasn't a single one of them who'd have felt gypped, neither, if he'd had his way with me. Now I'm all wore out and a nanny goat would make a prettier showing. And it's all your fault, Spence Douthit! You've worn my region to a frazzle!"

Spence waited for her to continue but, after remaining silent for several minutes, he decided she had finally talked herself into exhaustion. He put his feet on the floor, being careful not to make any sound, and listened. He could hear Maud's heavy breathing, and the hoarse rasping of her throat, and it made him feel a lot better.

He got up and tiptoed through the room where Maud lay. She had stretched herself out on the cot and she looked helpless and wan. She paid no attention to him as he went through the room to the door.

When Spence cautiously opened the bedroom door and peeped inside, Bubber was still asleep. Spence watched him a moment before opening the door any wider. After that he went inside and looked at the boy. Spence was surprised to see that, even though Bubber's mouth was partly open, the lines of his pimply sallow face were still set in the same foolish-looking grin. He scratched his head thoughtfully, wondering how he was going to be able to keep the boy there until he could find Mavis and bring her home. When he and Bubber got there between three and four o'clock that morning, Spence had promised to show him Mavis without fail when he woke up. Now he did not know what he was going to do. Bubber would probably wake up thinking he had been tricked and, discovering that Mavis was at The White Turkey or somewhere else, put on his clothes and leave before Spence could stop him. Spence looked around the room. Quickly gathering up Bubber's suit, shirt, and shoes, he rolled them into a bundle and carried them to the back porch, where he hid them under the steps.

Maud was sitting up in bed again when he got back. She had seen him run outside with the bundle of clothes, and she was curious to know what he was doing.

"Why's that door shut, Spence?" she asked. "Who's in there? Is it Mavis, after all? Or did Libby come back last night?"

He went to the bedroom door and opened it wide enough for Maud to see Bubber on the bed. Maud's mouth fell open, and Spence hastily closed the door. Then he went to the chair beside her cot.

"What in the world, Spence?" she asked in an awed whisper, her eyes becoming larger and larger. "Who is that man? Why didn't you tell me about him sooner? What's he doing there in the bed?"

"Didn't I say I was going to find somebody to marry Mavis?" he said good-naturedly, poking her in the stomach with his finger. "Well, that's him!"

"Where'd you find him, Spence?" she asked, tense with excitement. "Who is he?"

"It's Bubber something-or-other. But that don't matter right now. We can find out the rest of his name after it's all over. The big thing is that he is one of the rich men you hear tell about. Now, aint that something?"

"How does he make so much money?"

"I don't know, but that's the way it's done sometimes. He just happens to be one of the money-makers of the world. Some folks just naturally have the knack. It's people like us who somehow can't make money behave."

"Is Mavis married to him now?" she asked hopefully, nodding at the closed door.

"Not yet, they aint," he said. "But that won't take no time. It's the least part of it. The big part was finding him. I'm real proud of that."

Maud got up and ran to the door. She opened it carefully and took a good look at Bubber. He was stretched out on his back with his eyes closed and his mouth open. While she watched him, Bubber brushed away several house flies that had been crawling ticklishly over his stomach and scratched himself. Maud closed the door and went back to her cot.

"Mavis aint in bed with him," she stated anxiously. "Why aint she, Spence?"

"That's the trouble, Maud," he admitted sadly. "I just couldn't find Mavis. She went away somewhere and didn't come back. Everybody I asked about her said she'd be gone all night. I couldn't do nothing about that when she wasn't there."

"Why didn't you wait for her then?" Maud asked in a peeved tone of voice. "You could've done that."

"No, I couldn't, neither. Bubber said he wanted to sleep, and I figured the best thing was to bring him here where I could keep an eye on him. He's too good a haul to let get away. Besides, by having him right here in the house, the troublesome half of getting Mavis married is all taken care of."

"But what you going to do about her?"

"I was figuring on going back over there tonight and bringing her back. They told me she'd be sure to be back by tonight."

The door suddenly opened and Bubber stood looking at them with a bewildered expression on his grinning face. The peculiar-looking smile stretched from ear to ear.

"Hi, there!" he said, grinning at them. He rubbed his eyes with the backs of his hands and looked across the room again. "Is that her?" he asked, blinking his eyes at Maud. "Is that the one you were telling me about?"

Spence jumped up hastily and ran to Bubber.

"Now, just hold on here a minute, Bubber!" he said desperately as the boy tried to get away from him.

"Don't go and get all upset just because you see Maud. Maud aint the one! Maud's only her ma!"

"To hell with that!" Bubber cried. The silly-looking grin on his face disappeared for the first time. "You can't make me marry that old crow!" He jerked free of Spence's grip and ran back into the room. "Where's my clothes! Who took my pants! Everything's gone!"

"Now, just hold on and listen to reason, Bubber," Spence pleaded, trying to grip him by the arm. "You woke up here and got all flustered when you saw Maud. I grant you that Maud aint a pretty sight. But she aint the one! Mavis don't look like that at all!"

"Mavis!" Bubber shouted. "Is her name Mavis?"

"That's her, all right," Spence said. "Don't you like the name? I always thought it was a real pretty name for a girl."

"Well, I'll be damned!" Bubber shouted. "What kind of a joke is this, anyway? I know all about her, if she's the same one that's out at The White Turkey."

"That's her," Spence said. "Mavis is out there, all right. What's wrong about that, though?"

Bubber sat down on the side of the bed and stared dejectedly at the worn bare floor.

"You aint already married to her, are you, Bubber?" Spence asked.

"Hell, no!" Bubber shouted.

"Then everything's all right, son," Spence said elatedly. "That makes everything just fine and dandy!"

"Why does it?"

"Because if you aint, you'll soon be."

112

"Like hell I will! I'm getting out of here!"

He jumped up and ran to the door. Maud, who had been standing just outside the door, stepped up and grabbed him around the waist. With Spence's help, she hurled him back into the room. Bubber backed into a corner.

"You can't make me do it!" he yelled.

Maud smiled coyly.

"You can tell what a fine-looking girl Mavis is just by looking at me, because I'm her ma."

She and Spence stood before him, blocking his escape.

"It's going to work out as slick as a button if we can only keep him contented till Mavis gets here," Spence told her. "I've made up my mind to that." He chewed the tip of his tongue for a moment. "I know just the thing, Maud! I'll be right back in no time! You keep him in that corner!"

Spence ran through the house to the back porch. He stopped at the steps and listened intently. There was no sign of Chet's being at home, and he hurried across the yard and rapped loudly on the Mitchells' window.

Myrt stuck her head out the kitchen door.

"What's the matter?" she asked, wild-eyed.

"Come here, Myrt!" he ordered gruffly. "Come here like I say! Hurry!"

Myrt came as far as the porch steps.

"Chet aint home, is he?"

Myrt shook her head, still puzzled by his behavior.

"Then hurry on over to my house," Spence urged, grabbing her by the wrist and jerking her down the steps and across the yard. "Quit that holding back!" he said, giving her arm a violent tug as she tried to keep from being pulled.

"You'd better be careful with me," she warned him. "You know Chet. He won't stop at nothing if he gets mad."

"That aint nothing to what I'd do to him," Spence said, pulling her up his steps and into the house. "Some day when I don't have my hands full, I'm going to take him on, too."

He ran with her into the house, still holding her firmly by the wrist. When they reached the bedroom door, he flung it open and shoved Myrt inside. Maud, holding a big water pitcher in her hand, had Bubber backed against the wall.

"Now!" Spence shouted excitedly. "This'll do the trick!" He grabbed Myrt around the waist and pulled her towards Bubber. "It'll do two things at the same time. It'll keep Bubber satisfied to stay, and it'll help me get even with Chet. Come on, Maud!" He flung Myrt at Bubber and ran to the door. Maud went out of the room and he closed the door.

An instant later he turned the knob and stuck his head inside the room. "Now, you folks act sociable," he told Myrt and Bubber.

After locking the door, he and Maud listened breathlessly for some sound. They could hear neither Myrt nor Bubber say anything, and as far as Spence could determine, they had not moved. He smiled at Maud.

"That'll keep the wagon wheels rolling for a while," he told her. "There aint a thing to worry about now."

He could tell by the worried expression on Maud's face that she was not as confident as he was. She lay down on her cot without a word. Spence sat down in the chair.

"It's a good thing I thought about that when I did," he said, nodding his head at the closed door. "Myrt'll keep Bubber from getting restless if anything will."

"Well, I aint so sure," Maud said skeptically.

"Why aint you?"

"Because."

"If you knew Myrt like I do, you wouldn't talk like that. Myrt can be real sociable when she wants to."

Maud raised herself on her elbows to glare at him. She was about to speak when an automobile squeaked to a stop in front of the house. Somebody got out and slammed the door.

"If that's that female—" Maud cried.

Spence motioned for her to be quiet. Somebody was running on the hard sandy ground towards the house. Spence rose up from the chair and ran to the front door. An instant later he stepped back out of the way as Jim Howard Vance came into the room. Maud lay down again.

"Well, Jim boy!" Spence said enthusiastically. He got a grip on the boy's arm and clung to him. "I sure am glad to see you. I wanted to talk to you when you was here the other day, but you know what happened. Libby

115

gets her head set on something, and nothing can change it. Sit down in the chair, there, and make yourself comfortable."

"I haven't got time," Jim Howard protested, backing away from the chair. "I'm in a hurry."

"Did you slip out of the government hospital again?"

"Nope. Didn't have to this time. I got my medical discharge about an hour ago."

"Then what makes you in such a big hurry, Jim boy? I've been wanting to talk to somebody about Beaseley County every day since I've been down here."

Jim Howard glanced around the room. When he saw Maud on the cot, he nodded nervously to her.

"How're you, Mrs. Douthit?" he said.

Maud moved her head up and down several times.

"What's your hurry, Jim boy?" Spence insisted.

"Libby asked me to come and get some things that belong to her," he said quickly. "She told me to look in an old trunk."

"What for?" Spence demanded. "Is she moving out without coming back here herself?"

"Well, we're going to get married this afternoon," Jim Howard said, smiling a little while he looked first at Maud and then at Spence. "That's why I'm in such a hurry. I've got a taxi waiting outside for me."

"That's a mean thing to do," Spence said. "Libby's going back to Beaseley County and leave me and her Ma down here stranded. It's a real mean thing to do."

Jim Howard moved uneasily from where he was standing in the middle of the room. He backed towards the

116

closed bedroom door. Spence followed him across the floor.

"The other day when I was here you were fussing because Libby wasn't married," Jim Howard said. "Now that we're going to get married, you're kicking. You don't make sense, pop."

"You'd kick, too, if somebody who kept you from starving ran off and left you."

Jim Howard made no reply for several moments. He looked at Spence and Maud, shaking his head slowly, as though he could not make up his mind to say something he wanted to very badly. Spence nervously shifted the weight of his body from one foot to the other.

"Now there aint no use getting mad at me, Jim boy," Spence said. "It aint my fault that I have to live here in this place. You're putting all the blame on me for everything that's wrong in the world. You know yourself that poor people have to stay here because they don't have the money to pay rent to live in better places."

"Libby doesn't stay here. does she?"

"Well, no. But——"

"Then there must be a good reason for it."

"Libby always was hard-headed about what she wanted. When she gets a notion that she doesn't want to do something, nothing can make her. It was the same way about living here in Poor Boy. She just made up her mind she wasn't going to stay, and she didn't."

"Mavis went away, too, didn't she? Maybe for a different reason?"

"Well, yes. But——"

"You are all wrong, pop," Jim Howard said. He watched Spence, shaking his head slowly. "Neither Libby nor Mavis would've left here if Poor Boy had been a decent place to live in. The ones who own this land are to blame for not putting up better houses, and the city is to blame for not doing something about it. You know yourself it's nothing but a rat hole, and people can't live like human beings very long in a rat hole. If places like this don't get wiped off the map, I'll be sort of sorry I ever went to the war and had my eyes opened. You feel like all that shooting and fighting on the other side of the world didn't amount to much in the end when you come back and find Poor Boys scattered all around the country."

"I reckon you're right about that," Spence admitted. "But, still, I don't know what it's got to do with me. I aint to blame for Poor Boy. I'm just one of the poor people who has to live here."

"You can get out," Jim Howard said. "If everybody like you got out, there wouldn't be people living here, would there?"

"That's what I'm working on right this minute, Jim boy. Now, you stop worrying."

Jim Howard nodded shortly and went to the bedroom door. He was twisting the knob when Spence reached him.

"Now, just wait a minute," Spence said hurriedly. "Don't go in there yet."

"Why not?" he asked in surprise. "I've got to get Libby's clothes."

118

"Can't you sit on the porch and wait? You don't have to hurry away like this."

"We're getting married in half an hour. That'd make anybody be in a hurry."

He unbolted the lock and stepped into the next room. Spence was right behind him.

Myrt jumped up from the bed and tried to reach the door. Spence caught her by the arm.

"Where is he at?" he demanded roughly.

"He jumped out the window and ran!" she told him.

"Who did?" Jim Howard asked, puzzled.

"Never mind," Spence said. "Nobody you know, son. You go on and get the clothes out of the trunk."

While he was opening the trunk, Spence dragged Myrt into the next room. Maud was waiting.

"Why'd you let him get away?" Maud asked angrily.

"I couldn't help it," Myrt said fearfully.

"Why didn't you yell for me then?" Spence demanded.

Jim Howard hurried into the room with several of Libby's dresses over his arm.

"It's your fault, Myrt Mitchell!" Maud cried. "You wanted to do something mean, and so you let him get away!"

"What are you folks talking about, anyway?" Jim Howard asked. "Who got away?"

"He was a sort of stranger," Spence said, patting his arm. "Now you go on with your load of clothes and get married." He pushed Jim Howard through the front door and followed him across the porch. "This is only a little argument between neighbors, son."

He waited until the taxi passed out of sight down the street and then hurried into the house. Maud had Myrt backed into a corner.

"If you'd treated him right, he wouldn't have run off!" Maud was yelling. "It's all your fault! He was everything we had to count on, and now you've gone and spoiled it!"

CHAPTER NINE

MAVIS WAS STANDING IN THE DOORWAY squinting her eyes as she surveyed the room. When Spence looked up and saw her standing before him, he thought he had fallen asleep and was dreaming. She stepped into the room and looked around carefully before coming closer.

"Dogbite it, Mavis, is that you, sure enough?" he asked, rising from the chair.

She smiled back at him.

"It is you, aint it?"

"Hello, Papa," she said.

Spence ran to the cot and shook Maud.

"Maud! Wake up! Look who's here!"

"Where?" Maud asked, opening her eyes sleepily.

Spence had noticed at once that Mavis had changed very little during the time she had been away. She was still youthfully awkward, and her arms and legs dangled from her tall body as though she did not know what to do with them. She twisted one leg around the other and locked her hands behind her back. Mavis was dark-haired and slender like Libby, but she had neither Libby's blue-black hair nor her full rounded figure. Her slightly-large lips were constantly parted as though she were bewildered and, at the same time, fascinated by everything she saw and heard. She was thirteen that summer, but most persons seeing her for the first time would have thought she was seventeen or eighteen. One moment she was youthful and demure, the next moment mature and bold.

Spence ran to Mavis and urged her forward with sweeping motions of his arms.

"Mavis, honey!" Maud cried, rising on her elbows.

Mavis crossed the room awkwardly.

"How are you, Ma?" she asked, watching both parents suspiciously.

"Mavis, I could just cry, I'm that happy to see you!" Maud said, reaching for her daughter's hand.

Mavis sat down on the edge of the chair, still watching her father. Spence went to the foot of the cot.

"Did you see Bubber running down the street away from here in a big hurry?" he asked her.

"Bubber?" Mavis said, startled. "What was he doing here?"

"You know him?" Spence asked. "You know Bubber?"

"Is he a little dried-up squirt with a silly grin?"

"That's him, all right!" Spence said excitedly. "How do you know about him?" He paused for a moment. "I had it all fixed up for him and you to get married."

Mavis laughed. "That's a hot one!" she said. "Bubber got me the job at The White Turkey. He gets paid for every girl he brings in. Bubber promises to marry all the girls, and then he takes them to The White Turkey and collects from the boss. That's all the marrying Bubber ever does."

Spence stared dejectedly at the floor for a long time.

"Well, just the same, he makes a lot of money, and I still might be able to talk him into marrying you. I aint giving up yet, anyway. If I can find him, I'm going to bring him in. He might be hiding somewhere, and it might pay me to go out and look around after a while."

He started towards the door.

"Florabelle's out there on the front porch," Mavis said. "Don't scare her away, Papa."

"Who?"

"Florabelle. My girl friend. We go everywhere together."

"Well, bring her in here!" Spence said expansively. "That aint no way to treat company! Bring her in the house!"

Mavis went to the door.

"Come on in, Florabelle," she said, taking the girl by the hand and leading her into the room. "It's all right!"

A tall brown-haired girl who appeared to be about the same age as Mavis and, like her, wearing a low-neck cotton dress and cut-out sandals, walked in. She was not at all frightened by the strange faces and surroundings, and she was much more at ease than Mavis. She smiled boldly at Spence.

"Well, howdy, Miss," he said friendlily. "You're mighty welcome here. We aint had no worthwhile company in a real long time."

Spence tried to take his eyes from the girl, but each time he looked off in another direction he found himself distracted until he could look at her again. Florabelle sat down and crossed her legs carelessly. Spence took a good look at her long slender legs and went to the door. He remained there with his back turned for only a few moments. He came back and watched her uneasily.

"I reckon I'd better go out and look around before it's too late," he said to all three of them.

Florabelle smiled at him when he left the room, but he did not turn back. He walked out into the street and looked in both directions. There was no one on the street at that time of the day, and the sizzling sun blurred his vision. He walked to the canal at the end of the street and looked closely at the banks on both sides. There were tall weeds growing down to the water, but there were no trees or bushes, and it would be difficult for anyone to hide along the canal. A tug boat was puffing up from the gulf, but otherwise there was no sign of life anywhere. He waited until the tug had passed, and then he went down the street, looking right and left for some place where Bubber might be hiding. All the houses near by were built high off the ground to keep flood waters from reaching the floors, and by walking slowly along the street and stooping over a little, he could see all the way under the houses to the back yards. After going to the end of the street and back, he was ready to

124

give up. It was hot in the sun at that time of the day, and the enervating heat, together with all the excitement, had left him exhausted. Besides, he wanted to look at Florabelle again. He hurried back to the house.

"Did you see him, Spence?" Maud asked as soon as he walked through the door and took off his hat to wipe the perspiration from his forehead.

"He's gone, all right," he said, shaking his head at Maud and shyly watching Florabelle's leg bounce up and down as she swung it on her knee. "He's skipped away as sure as anything."

Spence sat down and fanned his face with his hat. Florabelle smiled at him again.

"Papa, what did you want to see me about?" Mavis asked.

He looked at her in amazement.

"How in the world did you know about that?" he asked. "Who told you?"

"Jerrie said you'd been to The White Turkey asking for me. At least, she said somebody was there last night asking where I was, and when she told me what you looked like, I knew it must be you. That's why I came." She looked at her mother, then back again at Spence. "I thought I'd better come find out what you wanted."

"Well, that's funny," he said, smiling at Mavis and Florabelle. "I wouldn't have thought she'd remember me at all. What else did she say about me, Mavis?"

Mavis glanced at Florabelle while both suppressed giggles.

"Nothing," Mavis said. "She didn't say anything else, Papa."

"Well," he said, looking down at his feet, "I don't reckon there was much else to say, anyhow." He looked at the cot to see what Maud was doing. "I just happened to be asking about you at the time."

"That's what Jerrie said," Mavis commented. She looked quickly at Florabelle, and both of them laughed. "Jerrie's a case! She really is!"

"She's what?" Spence asked, looking from one girl to the other.

"Oh, she's a mess," Mavis said, giggling. "She says the funniest things sometimes about her dates."

"If anybody was to ask me, I'd say she does some peculiar things, too." Spence stopped and looked at Maud. She was evidently not listening to what he was saying. "I'd never get used to all that slapping, for one thing."

"Jerrie always does that to all her dates," Mavis told him. "Some of them like it."

"Well, you can tell her for me that here's a somebody who don't," Spence said. "Then, besides that——"

Maud reached out and took Mavis' hand in hers. "I declare, honey, you being here does me more good than a visit from the preacher," she said as she squeezed and patted her daughter's hand. "I haven't felt this good in I don't know when. It seems like you came back just at the time that helped the most. I was sure feeling poorly before I woke up and saw you standing there at the door, honey."

"You still taking your tonic, Ma?"

126

"When I can get it, honey. It seems like I just can't keep enough of it on hand, though. The biggest bottle goes so fast these days, honey."

"Have you tried getting up lately?"

"Only a little while at a time, honey. I can't seem to stay on my feet for only a short spell. I just have to crawl back into bed and rest up all over again."

Spence leaned over and tapped Mavis on the leg with his finger.

"Now, about that friend of yours," he said. "I don't reckon she said anything else about me, did she?"

"Who?"

"He's talking about Jerrie," Florabelle spoke up. Both girls giggled.

"That's who I mean!" Spence said eagerly. "That's her!"

"I don't remember anything else. Do you, Florabelle?"

"She said it took both her and Mamie to get rid of him when she was through," Florabelle said. "Jerrie really does some funny things sometimes."

"I don't call none of that funny," Spence said curtly, his face scowling. "I do recall something about that old fat colored woman shoving me around, though. Neither of them would pay a speck of attention to what I wanted to do. I told them I wanted to stay right where I was till you got back, but they wouldn't hear to it. They said I couldn't stay in the boarding-house unless I had some more business to attend to there. Now, everybody knows good and well when you go there once, you're all through for a while to come. That old fat colored woman sure made me mad by the way she shoved me around out there."

"Florabelle and I were out on a party," Mavis said. "It lasted all night. That's why I didn't come back."

"Well, now that I can tell you about it," he said, "what I wanted to see you about was I wanted to get you to come home and see your ma before she took worse. I sort of figured you might be a little homesick, too, and would want to come back for a while."

Mavis was frightened.

"What you trying to make me do?" she asked, glancing at her father and then at the door.

"Nothing in particular. Your ma and me thought you might want to stay here at the house for a while. I wouldn't have thought about it if it hadn't been for the lady who came here talking about——"

"Not me!" she said in a loud voice. She moved her chair away from her father as though she expected to be caught in a trap any second. "I like it too much out at The White Turkey. I wouldn't leave there now for anything. Would we, Florabelle?"

Florabelle nodded faithfully.

"Now, honey, don't get yourself upset," Maud told her in soothing tones. She patted her daughter's hand. "All young girls have to think about marrying and settling down sooner or later. Your pa just happened to think it might be something that'd suit you. That's all, honey."

"But he aint going to make me stay here, is he?"

"Now, now, honey," she said reassuringly. "You just

quit thinking that. Nobody's going to make you do a single contrary thing. Just you don't worry now, honey."

"A fine home-loving husband never did no girl no harm," Spence said firmly. "And, of course, if he happens to have a little money in his pocket, or a good-paying job, it makes it even better. Now, if you was to take it into your head right this very minute to marry yourself a man like that in general, you wouldn't hear a single contrary word out of me or your ma. When a young girl like you finds out what it is she likes about the men, it pays to have a steady male around the house all the time, because then you don't have to get up and go out chasing every Tom, Dick, and Harry in all kinds of weather. There never was a better arrangement for a young girl than just that."

Mavis appeared to be more at ease by the time her father had finished, not because she had paid any attention to what Spence had said, but because she had laid her head on her mother's shoulder and closed her eyes with drowsiness.

"It's a mighty hot day, honey," Maud said tenderly, patting her arm and stroking her hair. "You ought to lay down and rest some. After being out in that hot sun, you must be plumb wore out. Both of you ought to go in the other room and take a nap till the heat cools off."

Mavis opened her eyes and looked at Florabelle drowsily through partly-closed lids.

"It sure would be nice to take a little nap, wouldn't it, Florabelle?" she asked languidly. "We didn't get a wink of sleep all last night."

"You can pull the shades down and make the room real cool," Maud said, running her fingers through Mavis' long hair. "It would be real nice, honey."

"Come on, Mavis," Florabelle said. She stood up and took Mavis by the hand. The two girls went to the door and looked at the room. "I could go to sleep and never wake up again," Florabelle said. They walked inside. "It's been ages since I've been in bed to sleep."

After they had closed the door and got into bed, Spence wandered in and out of the house aimlessly. Maud turned over and went to sleep, and Spence opened the bedroom door and went in. Both girls were sprawled on the bed talking and giggling about something in childish voices. Spence pulled aside one of the shades to see if they had opened the window.

"Now, you girls just take it easy," he said as he pushed the window up as far as it would go. "The hottest part of the day's coming on, and there aint a bit of sense in stirring around for a while."

As he walked past the bed he looked down and saw Florabelle smiling at him again. She looked even more tiny than she had appeared when he saw her for the first time. He leaned over the foot of the bed where he could get a good look at her.

"They sure-God do have a lot going on out there at The White Turkey, don't they?" he said to no one in particular while his eyes moved to and fro. "I never saw so much going on in all my life. All my money ran out before I got a chance to try my luck in a crap game, but

130

I did stand around the tables some before I left and watched the dice roll."

"Did you see the show?" Florabelle asked him.

"Did I!" he exclaimed. He sat down on the bed beside her. "I didn't miss! Dogbite it if that wasn't a sight!"

Mavis and Florabelle giggled childishly.

"It beats all get-out the way that girl with the little fur muff—" he stopped abruptly and looked down at Florabelle. Her body was shaking with laughter. "I never seen the like of that before," he concluded.

"We call that lifting-the-widow's-veil," Mavis told him seriously.

"Why do they call it that?"

Mavis and Florabelle looked at each other simultaneously and burst into giggles again.

"There must be a good reason for calling it that," he said as he watched Florabelle.

"It's just what it sounds like, I guess," Mavis said. "Florabelle does it better than anybody else. And she's been doing it for only a month, too."

"Is that right?" he said slowly, watching the girl. "Well, dogbite it!"

"Lifting-the-widow's-veil's not hard to learn," Florabelle said casually. "After the first few times it's real easy. I like to do it now."

Spence nodded to himself. Florabelle propped her head on a pillow and smiled up at him.

"You look like a mighty young girl to be staying away from home," he commented. "Don't your folks mind at all?"

She shook her head solemnly.

"Well, that's funny," he said. "I wouldn't say you're old enough to stay away like that."

"My daddy was killed in the war," she said, looking up at him appealingly. Her large brown eyes blinked almost imperceptibly. "My mama's gone away, too."

"Why didn't you go with her?"

"She wouldn't let me."

"Where'd she go to?"

"New Orleans."

"All by herself?"

"With a man."

"When's she coming back?"

"She's not."

"She's not?" he repeated in amazement, glancing at Mavis and then back again at Florabelle. "Why aint she?"

Mavis sat up in bed.

"Papa, don't keep on asking her questions like that," she begged. "It makes her feel bad, and sometimes she gets to crying when she thinks about it and can't stop. Leave her alone, Papa."

"Why, I don't mean no harm," he protested. "It just looks to me like nobody's got any business turning a girl her age loose in a big city. It aint so bad, somehow, for a grown woman to carry on in her way, but it don't seem right for any human to go away and leave a thirteen- or fourteen-year-old girl to scramble for herself. If I had the chance, I'd tell somebody like that a thing or two. It just aint right! No, sir, it aint!"

He got up and walked around the room. He was

132

angry. There were parents who allowed their children to run wild, but he had never heard of a woman turning a young girl out on the streets while she ran off to New Orleans with a man. He knew there never had been a time, regardless of how harassed he was by debts and poverty, when he would have turned Libby or Mavis out in the world to shift for themselves. He knew he was guilty of laziness and inability to make a living for his family, but he considered himself a saint in comparison with Florabelle's mother.

"Maybe it aint none of my business," he said as he walked back to the bed, "but a woman who'd do that ought to have the law after her."

"Mama told me how to get along without her," the girl said innocently.

"How in the world did she do that?"

"Before she went away, she took me to the movies and showed me how to pick up a man."

"To what?"

"Make a pick-up."

"And did you?"

"We picked up two men—one for me, and one for her. It was real easy."

"That's the quickest way to get in trouble that I know about," he said.

"She showed me how to protect myself," Florabelle said.

"Your own ma did that?" he asked.

Florabelle nodded.

Spence looked at her with a steady gaze, unable to

think of anything he could say and wishing her mother were there so he could tell her what he thought of her. Then and there, however, he made up his mind to do everything possible to get Mavis back to Beaseley County; if he could not find some one to marry her right away, he would do his best to find some other way to get the money for the trip.

"You don't have to look so worried," Florabelle said, teasing him. "I'm used to it now. I don't have a bit of trouble, and I get a man almost every time I try."

"You may be used to it," he told her roughly, "but I'll bet your daddy wouldn't be if he was alive and knew about it. It's a pity men with young daughters had to go off to the war and get killed. It just don't make things worthwhile in the end."

She began crying softly. Spence did not know she was crying until he saw that she had put her arms over her face and tried to keep from making any sound. When he looked at her, tears were rolling down her cheeks. He gazed at her pityingly.

"Now, look what you've gone and done, Papa!" Mavis scolded. "I told you she'd cry if you talked about her mama and daddy. Now you've gone and done it!"

Mavis put her arms around the sobbing girl and drew her against her bosom. Florabelle sobbed brokenly, pressing her face against Mavis and clinging to her like a frightened child seeking protection and comfort in her mother's arms.

"Every time somebody talks like that to her, she cries," Mavis said. She hugged the girl in her arms, stroking her

134

hair and holding her cheek close against her own. She held Florabelle as though she were a doll she loved very dearly and had cared for a long time. Florabelle responded gratefully to everything Mavis did. "Now, Papa," Mavis told him, "don't you ever say anything to her about her daddy again. She just can't bear to think about him."

Spence brushed the back of his hand over his eyes and moved away. He went to the window and stared blindly at the dusty sun-baked street. There he could still hear Mavis' soothing and comforting sounds as she rocked Florabelle in her arms.

He was about to leave the window when a car came up the street and stopped in front of the house. Spence glanced at it indifferently, but when he saw the door open, and Miss Saunders stepped out, he jumped with a start. He took another look to be sure it was Miss Saunders, and then he ran to the door.

"It's Miss Saunders!" he called excitedly to Mavis. "She's back just like she said!"

He hurried to the porch, slamming the bedroom door behind him.

CHAPTER TEN

MISS SAUNDERS, WEARING A KNEE-LENGTH, sleeveless, white linen dress, on the shoulders of which were pinned several black figures that had the appearance of galloping wild horses, and looking cool and unruffled in spite of the stifling midsummer heat, smiled uncertainly as she saw Spence hurrying down the path to her. Her blonde hair was piled on top of her head in a mass of curls and waves, and she reminded Spence of some of the high-school girls he had seen on the streets. She looked youthful and frightened.

Spence slowed down when he was half-way along the path. Miss Saunders had come no closer to the house than the sidewalk, and even at that distance from the dwelling she showed every sign of being ready to jump into her car and drive away the instant Maud appeared. Spence was out of breath when he reached her. He leaned against her sedan and tried to get his breath back.

"I seen you—" he said, panting. "I ran out here as

137

quick as I could—" He wiped his face with his shirt-sleeve. "Aint nothing to worry about——"

Miss Saunders nodded, but she continued watching for any sign of Maud about the house.

"Is your wife feeling better today, Mr. Douthit?" she asked. "I hope everything's all right now."

"Maud aint said an ugly word since this morning," he told her, "except for a few to me and some others to Myrt Mitchell, which don't count, because there aint nobody more aggravating than a Mitchell. It aint unusual for her to say some of them to me, because I'm used to them now."

"Well," Miss Saunders said, sighing a little and glancing at the front door, "I certainly hope you've explained my position to your wife. She should understand by now she has absolutely no cause to suspect my motives. You know yourself, Mr. Douthit," she said with a short laugh, "the last thing in the world a welfare worker would dream of doing would be carrying on a flirtation at a time like this. It just isn't done, you know."

"I don't know so much about that," he said, "because a young girl like you has to find a way to have a little fun somehow or other, and I don't blame you one bit for wanting to get some loving here and there, but what got Maud so upset was that she figured you was one of these women who come around ever so often with a little handbag selling neckties or such and then invite you to come down to some auto trailer camp and pay them a visit after dark. That's really where the money goes. It aint into the neckties."

138

Miss Saunders had been nodding her head during all the time Spence was talking and trying to make him understand that further explanation was unnecessary. She sighed with relief when he finished.

"Did you expect to see me back so soon, Mr. Douthit?" she hastened to speak.

"Dogbite it if I figured at all, Miss. I clear forgot all about it till I saw you drive up a minute ago. My mind's been taken up with a heap of things all day. I was in the house there just now talking——"

"You mean you didn't go after Mavis?"

"Oh, that!" he said with a laugh. "I thought you was talking about you coming back here to the house. No, sir! I didn't waste no time at all about the other. I got all dressed up last night and went out there to The White Turkey just like you told me to do."

"I'm glad," she said with a smile. "I knew you would cooperate, Mr. Douthit. We've depended so much on your cooperation that I couldn't bear to——"

"Dogbite it if that aint the sportingest place I was ever at! Why, you wouldn't believe it, Miss, but I was sitting down whiling away the time, when all of a sudden I looked up and here came a good-looking girl about seventeen or eighteen years old who had only a teeninecy little black fur muff——"

"Mr. Douthit!" she said quickly. "What on earth are you talking about?" She looked at him nervously, biting her lips as she tried to think what to say next.

"It's just like I said, Miss," he went on before she could stop him. "She had this teeninecy little fur muff in

139

front of her when she came out, and then it wasn't long before she was holding it over her head like it'd been a little umbrella or something."

He stopped when he realized she was shaking her head with a disapproving look. She was no longer smiling.

"I'm glad you took my advice to go out there and bring Mavis——"

"I sure-God have got you to thank for telling me about The White Turkey," he started again in spite of her efforts to stop him. "After I'd been there a while, I went out to the boarding-house with Jerrie——"

"Boarding-house?" she asked. "What's that?"

"I don't blame you for asking," he said. "I didn't know it by that name myself at first. That's just a name for the place where the girls——"

"Never mind, Mr. Douthit!" she said hastily. "We won't discuss that any more."

She was shaking her head disapprovingly again, and he could not find a trace of a smile on her face.

"I was only trying to tell you what I done——"

"I want to know what you did about your daughter, Mr. Douthit. That's my only reason for being here. I am not selling neckties, you know!"

He started to laugh, but she looked so stern that he thought better of it.

"Now," she said, speaking briskly, "you can tell me about Mavis, Mr. Douthit."

"Oh, she's right there in the house," he spoke up, pushing his thumb in the direction of the bedroom. "I'd bring her out here, but she's taking a nap right now."

"That's marvelous!" she cried joyously. She reached out for his hand and squeezed it excitedly. Her breasts rose and fell distractingly as her breath came in short gasps. "It's simply wonderful, Mr. Douthit! I'm so glad! I just knew you would cooperate with us. Mrs. Jouett is going to be so delighted when she hears about this. Mrs. Jouett, you know, was very skeptical from the start. She said she just knew it was hopeless to expect the least bit of cooperation from you. Of course, I've had complete faith in you from the beginning, and I told her I just knew I could count on you. Now, I can go to Mrs. Jouett and tell her what splendid cooperation we're receiving from you. It'll do so much to revive her faith in human nature. She has become awfully discouraged during the past year or so."

"You mean that woman with the long horse's face who came prowling around here the other day?"

"Mrs. Jouett, yes!" Miss Saunders said, almost dancing with eagerness. "She is such a splendid type of woman! She has given her whole life to social welfare work!"

Spence shook his head regretfully.

"If I'd known it was going to help her out any, I wouldn't have done it. I'd be satisfied to stay in my part of the world for the rest of time if it'd keep her in hers. God Himself, if He could see her now, would say she's the sorriest excuse for a female that ever squatted. There's about as much use for a woman like that as there is for a pig with a side-saddle. You know yourself a man would have to be mighty hard up to piddle around with her."

"Now, look here, Mr. Douthit!" Miss Saunders said

sharply. "There are some things you must not say in my presence. I'm not a prude by any means, but you can't talk that way about Mrs. Jouett!"

Spence glanced at her for a moment and lowered his gaze. He walked down the path to the porch and sat down on the steps, leaving Miss Saunders at the sidewalk. He could hear Mavis and Florabelle talking in excited whispers at the window behind his back, but he made no effort to hear what they were saying. He looked up to see Miss Saunders, looking meek and subdued, coming towards him. He said nothing when she stopped at the steps and looked down at him like a scolded child. After a while she sat down on the other end of the steps. He noticed that she was turned a little to one side so she could watch the door behind them.

"I didn't mean to speak so roughly, Mr. Douthit," she said apologetically. He could see from the corners of his eyes that she was looking down at the ground. "I'm sorry, Mr. Douthit," she said in a low voice.

Spence acknowledged her remarks by grunting gruffly and shuffling his feet on the sandy ground.

"It aint that so much as it is that other woman," he said. "It makes me want to get shed of the whole business when I think about helping her out. I'd do anything in God's green world for you, Miss, but I wouldn't even spit on the fires of hell if she was there and spitting would put them out."

"We are only trying to help, Mr. Douthit. You know that, don't you?"

"Sometimes I don't know," he said. "Jim Howard says

Poor Boy ought to be wiped off the map and all the people made to leave. Then you come along trying to get me to leave, but letting everybody else stay. It aint fair, somehow, to make me get out, and then to let the others stay. If you're going to do anything at all, you ought to treat everybody fair and square. Why don't you make Chet Mitchell leave, too? And all them other people down the street?"

"I'm afraid you don't understand, Mr. Douthit. The function of the Welfare Department is to administer to distress cases, not to depopulate the city completely."

"Then send some other department around here to Poor Boy and have it burned down, or something. I'm getting good and tired of being the only one in Poor Boy who has to leave. If I have to go, I want everybody else to go, too."

"Don't be selfish, Mr. Douthit. There are many persons in the neighborhood who are able to support themselves and their families."

"Sure! Chet Mitchell! He makes big money! Maybe I would too if I sold marijuana cigarettes wholesale like he does!"

"Now, Mr. Douthit, don't let yourself get upset. I have some very good news for you."

She reached over and patted his arm briefly with one hand while holding the neck of her dress together with the other. He could hear the excited whispers of the two girls behind the window curtain and he wondered what they were talking about.

"I called on your landlord this morning," Miss Saunders was saying, "and I made arrangements to have your past due rent taken care of."

Spence's mouth fell agape.

"What's that?" he asked. "What about the rent?"

"It's all been paid up, Mr. Douthit," she said with a wide smile. "You don't owe a penny of rent now. It's been paid up to the end of the month, which is tomorrow. Now, doesn't that make you feel a lot better?"

"It sure-God does, Miss," he said, "but I still don't see how it could be done. I owed the rent collector for three whole months, Miss."

"I know. But now everything's taken care of. You'll never have to worry about it again. Our Department rarely does a thing like that, except in extreme cases, but I'm so deeply interested in your case that I went to Mrs. —" She stopped and bit her lips. "I went to our director and said that your case was extreme and unusual, and recommended forthright and immediate action. Of course, this is my first case since I joined the Department, and I want so much to start off well. I thought if I could dispose of your case it would be of great help to my career. Naturally, I want to succeed from the start."

"Dogbite my pecker if I ever thought that'd happen! That rent's been hanging over my head for so long I'd just about decided it wasn't no use to worry about it no more. There sure-God is some fine people down here in this part of the world, after all. I'd already made up my mind that this place was where the worst folks bred. Now we can stay here and not have to worry about paying up! Let me go tell Maud——"

He was almost on his feet before she caught his arm and pulled him back.

"Please wait!" she said excitedly. "Let me finish what I want to tell you, Mr. Douthit. You should know the whole story before you tell your wife, because we must not let any kind of a misunderstanding come up now. That would be most unfortunate!"

Miss Saunders glanced at the door before continuing.

"We have a very good reason for clearing up the rent. Investigation revealed that you owed three months' rent, totaling forty-five dollars. There is also the matter of the water bill and the light bill, both of which are relatively small. We'll take care of those, too, of course. Now, the reason we are doing all this for you is because we want you to take your family back to your former home."

"Beaseley County?" he said, raising his voice to a high pitch.

"Yes, Beaseley County, if that's where you lived before moving down here. But please remember that we are not forcing you to move—we are merely offering you help so you won't have to stay here against your wishes. On the other hand, if you don't go, then we will be forced to stop the payment for the rent."

"You mean if I stay here you won't pay the rent?"

"That's right."

"That sounds to me like you don't want me to stay here," Spence said. "I thought all along you was just being big-hearted."

Miss Saunders had become nervous again. She leaned forward anxiously.

"Please don't misunderstand me, Mr. Douthit," she begged. "Of course, I like you, and I think you are a splendid person. But I do hope—well, I think you will be a lot happier back at your former home. Don't you see?"

He looked at her for several moments, during which time she leaned closer and patted his hand. He could see that she was waiting expectantly for him to decide what he was going to do.

"Well," he said finally, "I reckon I would like it better if I could go back to Beaseley County."

She squeezed his hand and smiled with relief.

"Oh, I'm so glad you decided to go, Mr. Douthit!"

Spence turned around and tried to see Mavis behind the curtains. He wanted to tell somebody about the great stroke of good fortune that had befallen him. He looked at the window again, but he could see neither Mavis nor Florabelle. He thought he heard them running across the floor.

"Now remember, Mr. Douthit," Miss Saunders said, "we are doing this with the clear understanding that you'll take Mavis with you. If it were not for her, we couldn't use our funds in this manner. And of course you'll take your oldest daughter, too."

"Don't worry about Libby. She's getting married right this very day to Jim Howard, and that makes her all taken care of. Anybody married to Jim Howard won't have to be worried about, because Jim Howard's got just as much sense as the next one to come along. He'll keep Libby out of trouble."

"That's splendid," she said. "In that case, it'll be much

easier for you to watch over Mavis. When you get back home, Mr. Douthit, let me suggest that you stay there. A city like this, with a population of nearly half a million persons, is no place for you or Mavis. The constant struggle to get the bare necessities of life is too much for some people. Besides that, there are many others who simply cannot resist the temptations a city this size offers. The wise thing for you to do is to go back home and stay there. If I were you, I'd never think of leaving home again. Above all, please don't come back here."

"I'd like it fine down here if I could find me a little job and make a big thing of it. The trouble is that I just can't get started on making a living since the powder plant closed down and dumped me here in Poor Boy."

"Well, that's all immaterial now, Mr. Douthit. You are leaving, and you won't have to live in Poor Boy another day. Tomorrow, bright and early, you'll be on your way home."

"I get to feeling sad when I start thinking about leaving," he said, looking off into the street. "Come to think of it, I sort of hate to go. Maybe if I put it off a while, in another month or two I'd change my mind again."

Miss Saunders closed her eyes for a moment. He could see that she was much more tired-looking than she had been only a few minutes before. While he watched her silently, she opened her eyes and, bending forward again, put her hand on his.

"Please, Mr. Douthit," she said wearily. "Please go home. For my sake, Mr. Douthit!"

Spence nodded.

"I don't suppose you have the money for bus fare, do you?" she asked, shaking her head as if she were prompting him. "You don't have it, do you?"

Spence shook his head as she was doing.

"I forgot about that part, Miss," he said. "I just aint got it, that's all."

She smiled and straightened up a little.

"I'll meet you at the bus station tomorrow morning and buy the tickets for you," she said, giving his hand a final pat. "Now, doesn't that make everything just splendid?"

"I aint used to having strange women pay out money for me," he told her sternly. "I couldn't do that."

"But it's a rule!" she cried nervously. "The Welfare Department never supplies transportation any other way. Mrs. Jouett wouldn't dream of having the case handled any other way!"

"Then I won't go," he said flatly. "I'll stay right where I'm at before I'll take money from a woman."

"Please, Mr. Douthit!" she begged.

Spence shook his head firmly.

"For my sake, Mr. Douthit! Do it this one time for me!"

"Nope."

"You won't?"

"Nope."

Miss Saunders took a deep breath and bent forward. She waited hopefully, watching his face. She could see him watching her from the corners of his eyes, and she

148

leaned closer. Slowly his head turned towards her. She waited for a long time before she dared speak again.

"Will you go if I leave the money for the bus tickets with you now?" she asked.

"That's different, Miss," he answered brightly. "I'd be pleased to hold the money till it came time to buy the tickets. I could do that, all right."

She sat up abruptly and opened her pocketbook. He watched her draw out a small roll of greenbacks.

"Here's thirty dollars, Mr. Douthit. I'm going to give it to you for the bus fare. However, I want you to know I'm breaking a hard and fast rule when I do this. Now, please promise me you'll buy the tickets!"

"Oh, I'll do that, Miss," he assured her as he reached for the money. He took the bills as though they were cobwebs that might disintegrate before his eyes if they were not handled carefully. He turned the roll of money over, inspecting it on all sides.

"Whatever you do, don't fail me, Mr. Douthit. If Mrs. Jouett ever found out that I had not bought the tickets myself, she would never forgive me. This is my first case since graduation, and I simply can't fail, because my career means so much to me. Now, I'd advise you to sell your furniture for whatever it will bring, and sell it as quickly as possible so you will be ready to leave in the morning. I'll be at the bus station waiting to see you off. The bus leaves at seven o'clock. Please don't fail me, Mr. Douthit!"

"I sure won't, Miss. And the best part of it is that I

won't have to fool around with Bubber no more. He ran away before I could——"

"Bubber? Who is that?"

"Bubber's the fellow who was going to marry Mavis before this big wind-fall happened. It was all fixed for him and Mavis to get married, and then he was going to let me have the money for the trip back to Beaseley County. He ran off a while ago, and I didn't know what I was going to do."

"It's a good thing he did run away, Mr. Douthit. Mavis is far too young to be getting married. It would be downright indecent at her age. I'm certainly glad I came here today."

"Me, too, Miss. It saves me a heap of worry over Bubber. He can stay gone now, for all I care. He sure was a half-witted fellow if I ever saw one. You ought to have seen him grin. He grinned every minute like a plain fool."

Miss Saunders got up and held out her hand. Spence gripped it tightly.

"Now, remember what I said," she reminded him. "All this has been done for you on condition that you take your family back to your former home."

"You don't have to worry none at all, Miss," he said, shaking her hand energetically. "It's something I won't forget as long as I live."

"Then don't forget to be at the bus station bright and early tomorrow morning. The bus leaves at seven sharp."

"I'll be there, Miss."

Before he finished, he saw Miss Saunders backing

away from him. Her eyes were wide and terrified, and her lips were trembling. He turned and looked behind him. Maud, hands on hips, and her pink nightgown falling in a roll around her waist, was glaring meanly at Miss Saunders. She did not say a word then, but Spence knew it would be only a matter of seconds before she yelled at Miss Saunders. He stuffed the roll of money into his pocket and followed Miss Saunders down the path to the street.

"What'd I tell you the last time?" Maud shouted.

"Now, Maud, hold your horses like I tell you," he spoke up authoritatively.

"You shut your mouth, Spence Douthit!" she told him in her loud angry voice.

Spence backed away, his anger vanishing.

Miss Saunders was half-way to the street by then, and she went a little faster as she got closer to her car.

"I've got a good mind to come out there and scratch your eyes out!" Maud shouted at her. "You didn't pay no attention to me when I told you to keep away from here, did you! I've been itching to get my hands on one of you son-of-a-bitching necktie sellers! I know all your tricks, because I've been watching every last one of you ever since you started coming around pretending to sell neckties. You aint fooling me none, though! I know what you're up to! You come around wagging your behind and get a man so worked up there aint no way in God's world for a good woman to satisfy him!"

Maud ran to the steps, and Miss Saunders dashed for her car. She hurled herself under the steeringwheel, and a moment later the car was roaring down the street in a cloud of dust. Spence, beyond Maud's reach, watched the dust drift out of sight. He had his hand in his pocket where he could feel the roll of money, but he was afraid to look at it while Maud was watching him. He waited until she went back into the house mumbling to herself.

CHAPTER ELEVEN

SPENCE SQUEEZED HIS FINGERS AROUND the roll of money until his palm was hot and moist. It was more money than he had seen, much less possessed, since the final payday at the powder plant. And now that he had so much money after all that time, he felt compelled to tell somebody about it. He ran inside the house.

"Maud!" he called excitedly. "Look here, Maud!"

She had lain down on her cot and pressed her face against the wall; when she turned over, her expression was angry and sullen. Spence sat down on the side of the cot and thrust out his hand at her, holding the money before her startled eyes.

"What's that?" she asked.

"It's money, Maud! Real honest-to-God money!"

"What's it for?"

"It's the wherewithal to take us home!"

"Where'd you get it?"

"The kind lady gave it to me. She even went and paid

up all the past due house rent, and then gave me this thirty dollars besides. Now, that's what I call real neighborliness. There aint many folks in the world who'd do a favor like that."

"Why'd she do it?"

"Why?"

"You heard me! Why?"

"Dogbite my pecker, Maud, what difference does it make why she done it!" he shouted impatiently. "Aint it enough that she went and done it? Besides, big windfalls don't happen every day in the year to folks like us. It's a real occasion!"

"It's a real suspicion to me," she said, poking the roll of money with her finger. Spence kept a firm grip on one end of the roll. "I wouldn't trust nothing about it."

She suddenly grabbed at the money, but Spence was on guard against just such a move, and he jerked it beyond her reach and held it behind his back.

"Oh, no, you don't!" he shouted as he pushed her down upon the cot. "I'm the cock of the roost around here when it comes to holding this money!"

Maud was sullen.

"I never saw or heard of anybody handing out free money and paying up the rent without reason. I don't like the looks of it."

"The kind lady just wanted to do us a kindly deed, Maud. There's people in the world who spend all their time doing nothing but kindly deeds. We just happened to be lucky enough to run spang into one of them. That's how it came about."

154

"I've got my suspicions of things that fall out of a clear blue sky," she said. "I aint no fool, Spence Douthit."

"I aint neither," he told her with a nod of his head. "That's why I'm holding on to it like I am."

Maud's lips tightened into a long thin line across her face. Spence pushed himself all the way down to the foot of the cot beyond her reach.

"We've been living on the backwaters all our lives, just like Jim Howard said, and never had a chance to run into folks like that before. Jim Howard went to the war and his eyes opened, and we came down here from Beaseley County and got ours opened. If there's one kind lady like her in the world, there's bound to be a lot of them, and from now on I'm going to stay on the look-out for them. It may be that another one will show up pretty soon, and after that, another one. A thing like that could keep up for a lifetime, and I've made up my mind I'm going to get everything that comes my way from now on. There aint no sense in doing without, when there's people who make a business of giving away money. Maybe from now on I won't ever have to worry about the rent and money for eating."

"You aint fooling me, Spence Douthit!" Maud said in a burst of anger. "That woman's out to be sported, and nothing else!" She threw the quilt aside and jumped to the floor. "I'll make her wish she didn't know a hard from a hoe-handle before I'm through with her! I've seen plenty like her in my time, and they're all out for the same thing. When it aint neckties, it's something else they're making a pretense about."

"Now, Maud, the lady aint even mentioned a thing like that since she's been coming here."

"Maybe she aint mentioned it, but she's acted it plenty!" Maud was glaring angrily.

"Dogbite it, Maud, don't get all feathered-out about a little thing like that. The kind lady only gave us the money because she wanted to help us out. She didn't even make one little bitsy speech about wanting something in return, except to say that Mavis could go along, too, if she wanted to. There's some fine folks down here in this part of the world that you'd never know about till you smoke them out. She's just one of them, that's all."

"She's just one of them daisies who's looking for a bee to buzz her!" Maud said in a shrill loud tone. "Those daisies don't fool me. I know all about it, because I've seen the time when I wanted to be buzzed, too!"

Spence stood up and walked cautiously across the room as Maud advanced towards him. He watched her hands as she swung her arms against her sides. He finally found himself backed against the wall.

"I'll kill that female if she comes prissing around here again like a bride looking for the bed in the dark!" Maud shouted into Spence's face. He could see both of her arms swinging threateningly before him. "If she knows what's good for her, she'll go after some other man, because you won't be no good for her after I brain the life out of you. There may be some woman who'll sit back and act dumb when a sporting female flits around like that one's been doing, but I aint one of them."

"Now, don't go and do nothing reckless, Maud," he begged.

"Reckless is what I'm going to do!" she replied. "I'm mad, and I mean what I say! The time's past when I'm going to stand back and look silly when there's a sporting female running loose. Do you hear me!"

"I hear every word you say, Maud," he pleaded. "Now, calm yourself and don't let a little thing like that get you all feathered-out."

She swung her forearm sharply against the side of his head. He had been expecting her to hit him, but he was surprised how much the blow hurt when it came. He put his arms over his face protectingly. Instead of hitting him again, which he expected her to do any moment, Maud stood in front of him, panting with exertion, and waited to see if he would try to run away from her. He kept both arms around his head while he squinted at her with one eye.

"Now, from now on, you keep away from that sporting female, Spence Douthit, or I'll brain you and her both as quick as I would a pesky housefly."

From the corner of his eye Spence could see that somebody was standing in the doorway. He waited until Maud looked as if she had decided not to hit him again, and then he turned his head enough to see who it was. It was Floyd Sharp.

"Come on in out of the heat of the day, Floyd!" he called urgently. "Walk right in, Floyd! I'm sure glad to see you!"

"What you folks fussing about?" Floyd asked, coming into the room and looking at them curiously. "What's gone wrong with you people?"

"Nothing, Floyd," Spence said quickly. "Nothing at all. Maud and me was just talking about something or other. I aint never too busy to stop what I'm doing and sit and visit with you, Floyd."

Spence waved his arm at Floyd, motioning to him to hurry inside. Floyd came part-way across the room.

"Talking, hell," he said, eying Maud suspiciously. "They call that bellowing where I come from. I could hear the noise a block away. I thought somebody was getting killed."

Maud gave Floyd a cold hard look. He returned the greeting by nodding at her a few times.

"I've had my say, Spence Douthit," she said, turning to him. "And you can just keep your mouth shut instead of trying to get Floyd Sharp to side with you."

"Jesus Christ, Mrs. Douthit," Floyd protested, "I was just curious, that's all. I aint butting in on something that don't concern me, because I know enough not to butt in on other folks' arguments. I got troubles of my own with my old woman. I wouldn't take on more."

Maud tossed her head and strolled haughtily to her cot. When she got there, she began searching under the quilt for her nightgown. Floyd watched her with absorbed attention.

"Where's Mavis?" Spence yelled. He ran to the bedroom door and looked inside. "She aint here! She's gone!"

Maud came to the door and looked for herself.

"What in the world's happened, Maud?" he asked, shaking with concern. "Mavis aint here."

"I reckon she just up and went," Maud replied, resigned. She shook her head as she turned away from the door. "I remember hearing both girls whispering and tiptoeing around the room only a little while ago. I told myself at the time that they was up to something, but I didn't think they'd be running off."

"I'll bet a pretty that Mavis heard us talking about going home," he said. "We was talking about it out on the porch, and then again in here, and she could've heard it all." He watched Maud helplessly. "That's what happened, as sure as anything."

"If there's one thing she don't want to do, it's to go back to Beaseley County," she agreed.

"Who's going to Beaseley County?" Floyd broke in.

"Us!" Spence said proudly. "We're getting ready to go back this very minute!"

"How you going to do that?" he asked skeptically.

"My house rent's all paid up, and I've got thirty dollars in cash money besides!"

"You're joking," Floyd said, looking from Spence to Maud. "Aint you joking?"

"We've made our plans," Maud said stiffly.

"Well, Jesus Christ!" Floyd said in amazement as he saw the superior smile on her face. "How'd that happen?" He turned and waited for Spence to speak.

"A kind lady who makes a habit of helping out folks in a bad jam done it," Spence stated proudly. He took

159

the roll of bills from his pocket and proudly showed it to Floyd. "There it is to prove I aint lying, Floyd!"

"Jesus Christ," Floyd muttered in awe. He poked the bills with his finger. "Just look at that money!"

"Aint no female going to give a pants-wearing man thirty dollars in cash money and not expect something for it in return," Maud said defiantly. She looked from one to the other as though she dared somebody to take issue with her.

"Well, this lady don't expect nothing," Spence said.

"Just let her try getting it off you," she told him. "I may be weak and puny, but I aint never been too weak to pull the hair out of a female like her. When I get through with her, it'll be a rainy day in a drouth before she comes prissing around my house again."

"Mrs. Douthit," Floyd said quickly, "if you don't want Spence taking money from her, just show her the way down to my house. My old woman aint that particular, even if she did find out what was going on."

"I'll attend to my own business, Floyd Sharp, and you attend to yours. If there's money passing around, I'll know how to take care of it without help from you. I don't appreciate strangers coming in here and telling me what to do, noway."

"Now, Mrs. Douthit, I didn't mean no harm. A fine-looking woman like you aint got a thing in the world to worry about. A fine-looking woman with your looks don't have to take a back seat for nobody."

Maud smiled coyly, and a pleased expression came to

her face. She tossed her head back and gazed down her nose at Spence.

"Well, did you hear that, Mr. Smarty?"

Stooping over daintily, she picked up her nightgown, threw it over her arm, and walked languidly out of the room and into the kitchen.

Floyd stared through the kitchen door long after Maud had passed from sight.

"Jesus Christ, but I wish my old woman had half the looks Mrs. Douthit's got," he said unhappily. Both of them turned and listened to Maud moving pans on the stove. "The more I think about it, the worse off I feel. I'm saddled down with my old woman to the end of time, and she gets to look worse every day. I reckon it's my own fault, though, because she was scrawny-assed before I married her, and I should've known what to expect from then on. I'll just have to make up my mind never to expect her to make as good a showing in front of a man as Mrs. Douthit does."

"Maud aint much for a sporting-minded man to look at after you've been around her as much as I have," he said in a depreciating tone. He unrolled the money and began counting the bills. "Ten, fifteen, twenty, twenty-five——"

"If there's a lucky man in Poor Boy, it's you," Floyd said enviously as he watched Spence flip the notes with his fingers. "You doggone Douthits sure do have the world by the tail. Jesus Christ! Nobody but a doggone Douthit would be lucky enough to have a strange woman give him money."

161

"Thirty dollars!" Spence announced proudly, folding the notes and putting the money into his pocket. "And every dollar of it real money, too!"

Floyd moved to Spence's side after a hurried glance at the kitchen door.

"What did you do to get that, Spence?" he whispered in his ear. "I can do anything you can."

"Nothing, much," Spence said.

"Where'd it all happen?" he asked, watching the door.

"Out there in the front yard," Spence said, twirling his thumb in that direction.

Floyd stepped back and looked at him harshly.

"The front yard! Now I know you're lying!"

"I aint lying, neither," Spence said emphatically. "I stood out there and held out my hand for it. That's all there was to it."

"And she just gave you the money, like that? You didn't hide out with her in the weeds, or nothing?"

"That's right."

"Jesus Christ, if that aint something!"

"To start with, I had to promise to take Mavis back with me. But now she's run off, and I'm in a sorry fix."

"Maybe she'll come back."

"She wants to stay here," Spence said shaking his head. "That's why she ran away like she done. For a while here I didn't know if she was coming at all, and I was upset because I had Bubber waiting to marry her. Then he up and ran off, but then Mavis turned up. Now, when I need Mavis for something else, she's gone."

"Bubber? Who's that?"

"Bubber's the silly-looking fellow I was keeping here

162

till he jumped out the window and got away. He skipped out and left his clothes behind, but he can't get far away looking like that."

"Jesus Christ, Spence. I caught somebody like that hiding in that little woodshed behind my house. He was scared to death, but he grinned all the time, anyway, and I told him he could stay till it got dark. He's down there now. I didn't see no sense in turning him out naked in the daylight. It must be the same one, all right."

"Well, I don't need him no more," Spence said. He thought about the matter for a while. "It does seem a shame not to make some use of him, though. After all the trouble I went to, he ought to be made to earn it back. Could you use him, Floyd?"

"Use him how?"

"The same way I was figuring on doing. Marrying him to one of your daughters, and then turning right around and asking him for some money that'd take you back home."

"Justine's the oldest, and she's only coming on twelve. I'd be scared to do a thing like that. I don't want to get into trouble."

"What about your old lady?"

Floyd shook his head.

"That wouldn't do, because I'd never find another woman to marry me in the fix I'm in."

Spence picked up one of the chairs and inspected it critically. The split-cane bottom was broken and frayed, but otherwise it was in fair condition.

"If you don't want to use Bubber, maybe you'll want this furniture of mine. I aint got no more use for it, be-

163

cause we're leaving here tomorrow morning at seven sharp." Spence went into the bedroom with Floyd following at his heels. "How'd you like to have a fine big double-bed, Floyd? It won't cost you much, because I aint hard up like I once was. You can have the big bed, and the two little cots, the radio, the chairs, and all the other odds and ends for scarcely nothing."

Floyd sat down on the bed and bounced his body on the mattress. He pulled back the sheet and looked at the ticking.

"How much you asking?"

"Nothing to speak of, Floyd. I've got to get shed of all this furniture right away, and you can name your own price. I wouldn't want to hold you up at a time like this, considering how friendly we've always been."

"I couldn't pay much, whether we was friendly or not," Floyd said.

"I couldn't ask much. You just set your own price. The main thing is for me to get shed of all these things so I can leave in the morning without a hitch."

"Well, if it'll help you out like you say it will, I'll buy it off you," Floyd agreed. "Of course, I aint got no money on me right now."

"How about that little store of yours?" Spence suggested. "You keep a little money on hand to run that, don't you?"

"There's a few dollars hid away somewhere about the house," he admitted. "I keep it hid for something important that might come up."

"I'll trust you till you get home," Spence said. "You

carry a load of furniture down there, look around for the money, and then come back for another load. You can give it to me then." Spence thought about the money for a moment. "Maybe it'll be better if I go down there with you, Floyd, and you can give it to me right away."

"Would four or five dollars be about right?" Floyd asked in a low voice.

"Four or five dollars!" Spence repeated loudly. "That aint no money at all. Why, this furniture cost me a heap more than that when I was working at the powder plant."

"But you aint working there now," Floyd reminded him. "Times have changed a lot since then. A few dollars, like four or five, is a pile of money in Poor Boy these days."

Spence nodded reluctantly. "I forgot about this still being Poor Boy," he said. "Since the lady handed me the thirty dollars, I've let my mind travel. You go on and take the furniture at your price, Floyd. I've got this thirty dollars in my pocket, and I can afford to let it go cheap."

Floyd threw the mattress off the bed, then the springs, and began dismantling the railings. When he had taken the bed apart, he loaded himself with all he could carry and staggered through the house to the porch. Spence picked up a couple of chairs, the radio, and the foot of the bed and followed him to the street. They went towards Floyd's house with the heavy furniture on their backs, weaving from one side of the street to the other while the neighbors wondered how Spence had managed to keep that much furniture as long as he had.

CHAPTER TWELVE

IT WAS LATE IN THE AFTERNOON WHEN they finished carrying all the furniture down to Floyd's house. The only thing Spence had left behind was the kitchen stove and, that being the property of the landlord, he was afraid to let Floyd take it away. When it came time to take the cot Maud was sleeping on, she had protested violently, calling both of them all the names she could think of. Spence had tried to argue with her at first, pointing out that he had to sell the furniture before they left, but when he realized nothing he said made the slightest impression on her, he grabbed her around the waist and held her while Floyd picked up the cot and ran out of the house with it. Maud was left with only a pile of old clothes to lie on and, when she began complaining about that, he told her that she could afford to do without a cot just for one night since they were leaving bright and early the next morning. However, the prospect of leaving and going back to Beaseley County did not take the place of the cot in her mind, and she continued to scream and scratch until she was too weak to fight for her bed any longer. After that was over, Spence went to the back yard and took Bubber's clothes from the hiding place under the porch steps. He hurried down to Floyd's house, and then waited in the yard while Floyd was arranging the new furniture the way he wanted it in the two rooms. He had trouble making the big double-bed fit into the room with all the other beds and cots, and it was not until he thought of loosening one of the walls by prying it from the sill and pushing it out about a foot from the floor that he was able to make the bed stand on all four legs. When that was done, he came out where Spence was waiting.

"This is the first time I ever had enough beds in the house for everybody to find a place to sleep at the same time," Floyd said as he sat down on the edge of the porch. The sun was sinking, and the golden glow softened the deep lines that had been carved into his face by worry and anxiety. Spence watched him with a feeling of deep compassion. Floyd was one person he knew whose struggle for existence was more hopeless and dispiriting than his. "But, considering how fast they come along, it won't be no time at all before the next batch of young ones crowd us again." Floyd turned his head and watched the fiery segment on the horizon. "I sure-God wish there was some way to make my old woman stop for a while. At this rate, another ten years will see me with more daughters than any two men put together ever had. When I think about it at a time like this, all I can say is that it's a curse God puts on a poor man. A rich man is more apt to have his children turn out to be boys. A poor man like me gets the girls. It just aint fair."

"The very same thing happened to me," Spence agreed. "The only thing is that I never could figure out whether I got girls because I was poor, or whether I got poor because I had girls. Either way you look at it, though, it turns out to be the same in the end. It sure does look like poor folks like me and you catch hell no matter what we do, and that's why I've just about decided not to do nothing no more. It just aint worthwhile to spend a lifetime struggling and grunting when we're going to end up worse off in the end, anyhow."

Both were silent after that for a long time. When the sun finally disappeared from sight, Spence got up and rolled the bundle of clothes into a tight round ball. Tucking the bundle under his arm, he started for the little shed behind the house.

"I want to get rid of Bubber's clothes," he told Floyd. "Bubber can't do me no good now, and I'll be satisfied to let him have all his things back so he can go on home."

Floyd got up and followed Spence around the corner of the house and through the rank growth of weeds that surrounded the shed. The shed door was closed and, before opening it, Spence stepped up to the window and looked inside. He could not see anything at first, so he wiped the dust from the pane and looked again. The bundle of clothes fell to the ground as he pressed his face against the glass.

"What's the matter?" Floyd said in a low whisper.

Without taking his eyes away, he began waving his hand at Floyd with quick excited motions.

"Come here, Floyd—quick!" he whispered.

Floyd stepped up to the window, flattening his nose against the pane.

"You see that?" Spence asked, digging his elbow into Floyd's side.

Floyd wiped some of the dust from the glass and looked again before he answered.

"It's Justine!" Floyd said with a quaver in his voice as he turned and looked into Spence's face. "It's her, all right!"

Floyd started to the door, but Spence grabbed him by the arm.

"Now, wait a minute, Floyd," Spence said. "You'd better not bust in there like that. He might do something desperate." He shook his head at Floyd. "Let's figure out——"

"Jesus Christ, there aint nothing to figure out, except what I'm going to do to him!" Floyd said.

"You'd better not do nothing till you know what you're doing, Floyd," Spence warned him. "Some people have spent a lifetime getting over what they done in too much of a hurry. You aint been in trouble down here yet, and you don't want to spoil it all, Floyd."

He could see Floyd's face twitch nervously in the fading twilight. His fingers were twisting a button on his shirt. Spence gripped his arm tighter.

"Jesus, Spence, I know what I'm doing!" he said. "There aint nothing I can do that'll be too bad for a man

170

who'd treat a little girl that way!" His eyes were cold and narrow as he stopped and looked at the button that had fallen into his hand. "I wouldn't stop at nothing now!"

"Maybe it aint all Bubber's fault, Floyd," Spence said. "Maybe she—maybe Justine——"

"That aint got a thing to do with it. It's what happens everytime the poor run up against the rich. I've seen it happen too often every way you can think of not to know it when I see it right in my own back yard. This is one time I'm going to put a stop to it!"

Floyd got loose from Spence and ran to the end of the shed where he picked up the axe from a block of wood. Darkness was rapidly closing in, and Spence could see several of Floyd's small daughters standing around the kitchen stove in the lighted kitchen a few yards away.

"Now, hold on, Floyd!" he begged, trying to take the axe from Floyd's hand. "Don't do something you'll be sorry about afterward!"

Floyd shoved Spence away roughly.

"I aint never going to be sorry from this time on," he said as he flung open the shed door. He disappeared inside, and Spence hurried in behind him.

Justine screamed childishly. "Daddy!" she cried.

"Get out of the way, Justine!" he ordered her. "Get in that corner and stay there!"

Spence saw Justine run from Bubber and crouch fearfully in the corner. She was stuffing the hem of her dress into her mouth while tears streamed down her face. Bubber jumped to the opposite corner. The boy's habitual smile looked as if it had been frozen on his face. His eyes were round and bulging with terror.

"Please, mister!" Bubber begged as he pushed himself against the wall. "Please, mister, don't hurt me! It aint my fault. Honest to God, it aint my fault. She came out here and asked me for fifty cents. I told her I didn't have a dime, but she kept on. I didn't start it—she did! Ask her, mister. Please ask her! Make her tell you the truth, mister! Please, mister!"

Floyd turned and looked around at his daughter huddled in the corner. She had stuffed so much of her dress into her mouth that not a sound was heard from her. The tears continued streaming down her face.

"For God's sake make her tell you, mister," Bubber sobbed. He dug his knuckles into his eye-sockets in a desperate effort to keep tears from blinding him. "Please make her tell you the truth. I didn't try to get her to do anything. She's the one who said she wanted to. It wasn't me, mister. You've got to believe me. I told her I didn't have any money. Please don't hurt me with that axe, mister—for God's sake don't hurt me!"

Bubber was still pleading when Floyd drew back the axe and swung it at him. The blunt flat head struck Bubber solidly above the temple, and almost immediately the boy sank with a feeble moan to the shed floor. Floyd raised the axe a second time and held it poised over his head while he waited for some sign of life in the body. Presently Floyd dropped the axe and walked to the door.

172

"Good God Almighty, Floyd!" Spence said, shaking all over with fear and nervousness. "Good God Almighty!" he repeated over and over again.

Floyd stood in the doorway facing the interior of the shed while his eyes moved back and forth as he looked from Bubber's motionless body to his daughter. His hands began to tremble, and he leaned against the doorframe for support.

"I aint sorry," Floyd said in an even tone as though speaking to himself. "I aint a bit sorry, now that it's done. I aint sorry at all. I'd do it all over again if I had to."

Justine was clawing at her face and trying to pull the cotton dress from her mouth. She had pushed so much of it into her mouth that she was choking and unable to breathe. Floyd went to her and carefully pulled the cloth out. Then he helped her slip the dress over her head and button the collar. After that he put his arms around her and held her while she cried brokenly.

"Please don't beat me!" she begged hysterically. "Please don't, Daddy. I won't do it again. I'll never do it again. Please don't beat me! That's the last time, Daddy!"

Floyd wiped the tears from her face and hugged her tenderly in his arms.

"My little girl," he said, stroking her hair and face. "My precious little girl. My darling precious little girl. Justine—Justine—Justine——"

"I promise, Daddy!" she cried gratefully. "I promise, Daddy! Please, Daddy, I promise!"

Floyd lifted Justine to her feet and guided her through

the door out into the starry moonlit night. She clung to him, still crying softly, until he turned her towards the lighted kitchen.

"Go in the house and eat your supper, Justine," he told her, giving her a gentle shove.

"All right, Daddy," she said as she ran through the weeds. He watched her until she entered the house, and then he walked slowly back to the shed. It was dark by that time, but the bright moonlight enabled him to find his way into the shed. Spence followed him inside and waited while he struck a match and held it over Bubber's body. The match-flame scorched Floyd's fingers and he shook it until the light was out. Spence waited to find out what he was going to do.

Floyd struck another match.

"Floyd," Spence asked, "what you figure on doing?"

"I've got to think about it first," he said calmly. "Before I can do anything, I've got to stop thinking about what he made Justine do. This never'd happened if I'd drowned every last one of them like I said. I waited too long, that's all. I knew it was going to happen sooner or later, because she's been on the streets asking men for money all summer. I knew about it, and it's my fault that I didn't take her and the rest over to the canal and do like I said. I'm to blame for it. I waited too long."

"Right now you'd better get busy and do something about him, first," Spence said, agitated. "You can't just leave him there like that."

"He's dead, aint he?" Floyd said dazedly.

"He's deader than a doornail," Spence said. "And

174

you've got to do something about him. He can't stay here."

"I've got to get rid of him, for sure. They might catch up with me sooner or later, but right now I don't care what they do to me. I've done my duty."

He walked outside and stood in the moonlight. Spence waited in the doorway and watched the children playing in the kitchen. He saw Justine come to the window and look towards the shed for a brief moment.

"I reckon this is just the beginning," Floyd was saying. "There's all those others coming along who'll be doing the same thing before long. As fast as they get to be eleven or twelve, I've got to expect it. There just aint no way to stop it that I know about, not as long as I have to keep them here in Poor Boy, anyway. They'll go on the streets just like Justine, and once they start taking money from men, there aint no end to what they'll do after that." He turned around and looked at Spence. "Spence, the worst plague God can put on a man is to make him poor and give him a houseful of daughters like I've got."

He went back into the shed and struck another match. Spence could hear him grunt as he lifted Bubber's heavy body and dragged it outside.

"You stay here, Spence," he directed. "I'll attend to this part. I don't want to get you mixed up in something that aint none of your business. You wait right here till I come back. I won't be gone long."

He went off into the night with Bubber's body slung over his back. Spence could see him wading knee-deep

175

through the weeds as he made his way towards the canal a hundred yards away. Some dogs were barking up the canal, but they were not close enough to do any harm. The nearest house, other than Floyd's, was fifty yards away in the opposite direction, and none of the neighbors could see what was taking place.

Spence sat down on the ground and leaned back against the shed to wait for Floyd. He listened to the barking dogs. He told himself that he would have done the same thing if Justine had been his daughter, but as he thought about it, he began to wonder if he actually could have brought himself to the point of killing a human being. He could not blame Floyd for what he had done, and he knew that no matter what happened, he would never speak about it to anyone else, but he could not keep from feeling that Floyd's killing of Bubber was useless and would not help matters to any great extent. As long as the young girls lived in Poor Boy there would be other men to tempt them with money and presents; when they became twelve or thirteen, they would run away from home just as Mavis had. By that time the habit of asking men for money would be so strongly rooted that they would never outgrow it as long as they lived. Spence shook his head wearily. He could not see any sense in trying to maintain beliefs to live by when he had no control over his existence, for no matter how strongly he struggled against fate, he was never able to master it. At the same time, however, he could not keep from admiring Floyd's attempt to change the course of his existence; but regardless of Floyd's success or failure, Spence still believed that life in Poor Boy was as easy to predict as the rising and setting of the sun, and that even murder could do little to change it. By accepting poverty as inevitable, he was resigned to living out the remainder of his years, either in Poor Boy or in Beaseley County, on bounty or luck. He was sorry Floyd had not come to the same conclusion before killing Bubber; Floyd had committed a crime in a futile rebellion against his poverty.

He heard Floyd wading through the weeds, and he jumped up. Floyd was short of breath after the hurried walk back from the canal.

"What happened, Floyd?" he asked.

"I dumped him in the canal," Floyd said, pausing for breath. "The current's pretty strong tonight and it ought to carry him away, even if the tide won't. He may be all the way out into the Gulf by morning."

"You see anybody—anybody see you?"

"Not that I know of." He leaned against the side of the shed. "We're the only ones who know about it, Spence."

"Justine was here when it happened. Don't forget that. She knows about it."

"I'll talk to her. After that, she won't tell anybody. I aint afraid of that."

"You don't have to worry about me, Floyd," he said quickly. "There's nothing or nobody who could make me tell."

Floyd nodded but said nothing. He turned his head a little to one side and gazed through the moonlight in the direction of the canal. The dogs had quieted down and there were no sounds near by. He straightened up after a while and went into the shed. When he came out, he was carrying the axe.

"I can't afford to let this go," he said, looking at Spence. "I wouldn't be able to buy another one, and I've got to have something to chop stovewood."

He struck a match and examined the axe-head.

"I'm going to keep it," he said decisively. "There aint a thing on it to show what happened."

Without waiting for Spence to say anything one way or the other, he carried it to the block of wood. Coming back he stumbled over the bundle of clothing near the window.

"Here's those clothes you brought down here, Spence," he said, kicking the bundle towards Spence.

"I'll get shed of them," he said as he picked up the bundle. "They can be put in the canal, too."

"I'll walk over there with you," Floyd said, coming behind.

They waded through the knee-high weeds as noiselessly as they could, neither speaking along the way. When they got to the bank, Spence hurled the bundle as far over the water as possible. The tight roll splashed faintly somewhere in the canal, and after that there was no sound other than the gentle lapping of the murky water against the bank. Floyd touched Spence's arm, and they walked single-file through the weeds to the house. Nothing was said until they were in Floyd's yard.

"What you going to do now, eat supper?" Spence asked uneasily.

178

"No. I aint hungry tonight. I'd rather go without." He sat down on the edge of the porch. "I'm a little shaky, Spence. I just can't help it. I feel like taking a walk somewhere."

"Me, too," Spence said promptly. He was anxious to get away from Floyd's house. "Walking'll help."

They went out into the street and turned towards town. They went in silence, walking rapidly and keeping close together. They reached the first cluster of stores, and Floyd stopped in the shadow of a tree. The street lights seemed brighter than usual.

"What's the matter, Floyd?"

"That sort of done something to me, Spence." He was breathing in short gasps. "Maybe I did the wrong thing, after all."

"I wish Jim Howard was here. He's got a lot of sense. He'd know the best thing to do."

"Who's that, Spence?"

"The soldier-boy from Beaseley County who's marrying Libby. Jim Howard went off to war, and he thinks Poor Boy's a rat hole, and worse, just like you do, Floyd. You and him together ought to be able to figure out a lot of things."

"That won't help none now, because I've already killed Bubber. I never killed a man before, and I hate to think I killed somebody. What I did won't stop Justine, or none of the others, in the end. Justine'll slip away from home and do the same thing again when she gets a chance." He looked at Spence helplessly. "I wish I hadn't done it, Spence."

179

"Once he's dead, he's going to stay dead."

"Jesus Christ, that's the trouble! I wish I hadn't done it."

Spence took him by the arm and led him down the street towards town. Floyd walked along beside him as if in a daze, and when they reached the corner, Spence had to take him by the arm and turn him in the right direction.

"Let's go down to Bill Tarrant's club," Spence suggested. "I've got money—thirty dollars of it."

Floyd walked along beside him for several minutes without speaking again. They were almost at Bill Tarrant's when Floyd stopped again and leaned against a tree.

"You're leaving here tomorrow," he said. "You won't be here no more after that."

"That's right," Spence said. "It's going to be a great day for me. Something like it'll turn up for you one of these days, Floyd. You just keep your eyes open."

Floyd looked him straight in the eyes and shook his head firmly.

"It won't happen to me," he said. "All of us in Poor Boy can't get our debts paid up and be handed thirty dollars, Spence. There just aint enough money in the world to do that for everybody, or if there is, nobody's going to take the trouble to do it for folks like me. The stroke of luck that hit you aint big enough to hit all the poor folks in the world. The only thing that'll help us any will be for somebody to come along and wipe Poor Boy off the map. And the only way to make somebody do that, is to get up and make a big fuss about it. With

180

that gone, there wouldn't be no need for me to worry about my little girls, because we'd all be someplace else where I could make a decent living for them."

"It might work if you could find a way to make a big fuss," Spence agreed, "but I don't know a single way to do it. If you got up in the middle of the street and shouted it out, they'd be sure to throw you in jail. Then you wouldn't be no better off, Floyd."

"That's what I'm thinking about. I don't know how, but I'm going to find a way. I just can't go on like this the rest of my life killing people because my girls grow up and start walking the streets. If I did, I'd be caught sooner or later, and then they'd start a lot quicker with me not around."

They walked down the alley and opened the door at Bill Tarrant's club. Floyd pulled his hat down over his eyes and followed Spence to the bar. They both called for bourbon-and-beer.

"I was thinking of going out to The White Turkey again tonight," Spence told him, "but if I can double my money here in the crap game, I'll be satisfied." He took out the roll of bills and peeled off five dollars to pay for the drinks the bartender was placing before them. He rolled fifteen dollars into a tight fold and put the money into his watch-pocket. "I'm going to try to double this other part first," he told Floyd, "and if that works out, I'll go to work and double this money in my watch-pocket. I'd hate to lose every penny of it on the first roll of the dice. It's too much of a risk that way. Come on."

They walked over to one of the crap tables and watched the dice roll several times. Presently Spence took out his money and counted it again.

"We'll never get rich if we don't work for it," he told Floyd. "Here, you take this dollar and see if you can't run it up into the real big money."

Floyd changed the dollar into four quarters and laid one of them on the pass line. Spence finished his drink and shouldered his way through the crowd to the other crap table. He turned his hat around backwards on his head and laid a dollar on the line.

CHAPTER THIRTEEN

By THE MIDDLE OF THE NEXT AFTERNOON
when he got back to the house wearing a new wide-
brimmed felt hat, for which he had paid four dollars, and
carrying over his shoulder a flour sack containing several
bottles of bourbon, beer, and stomach tonic, in addition
to a big brown alligator purse for Maud, which had cost
three dollars, Spence was beginning to worry.

For one thing, he had had a streak of bad luck at Bill
Tarrant's. At midnight he was twenty dollars ahead, but
shortly after that he began losing consistently, and two
hours later the twenty dollars was gone, and all he had
left was the money he had put into his watch-pocket
earlier in the evening. Floyd had persuaded him not to
touch that fifteen dollars by arguing that he would never
get home to Beaseley County if he lost it in the crap
game.

And that morning all except a few dollars of that had
slipped through his fingers so fast he could not recall ex-

actly how it had been spent. He had fully intended going to the bus station to buy the tickets, but there was so little of the thirty dollars left that he did not even bother to stop when he passed it on the way home. He had spent the night, or what was left of the night after Floyd finally went home, on the receiving platform behind a grocery store. It was after three o'clock in the morning when he and Floyd left Bill Tarrant's club, and since there were no beds left in the house, anyway, he had decided to stay down town and wait for the stores to open. He tried to get a few hours' sleep on the platform, but the concrete was hard and his mind was racing with worry. He had promised Miss Saunders to leave town at seven o'clock that morning. More than that, he had promised to take Mavis with him. He knew the fifteen dollars would not buy three bus tickets, but he told himself that it would be better for Maud and himself to go, or even himself alone, than it would be for all three of them to stay after Miss Saunders had put herself to so much trouble. It was dawn when he was able to close his eyes and go to sleep, but soon after that a Negro porter came to work and told Spence he would have to get up so the receiving platform could be swept before the manager arrived to open the store. He got a cup of coffee at a café, and after that decided to buy himself a new hat. He had needed a new hat for a long time.

When Floyd left Spence at three o'clock, he had promised to look around the house and do his best to find the few dollars he owed for the furniture. Spence had figured that if Floyd gave him four or five dollars, he could put it with the fifteen he had then and still be able to buy three bus tickets. By morning, though, after he had had a cup of coffee, he decided that the trip might be too hard on Maud in her sickly condition. There was a chance that she might die on the bus. He told himself that he could stand the trip back to Beaseley County better than she could.

While he was buying the hat and purse that morning, Spence had tried to shake hands with everybody he saw. Some of the men he shook hands with did not know him by name, but most of them recognized him by his clothes as somebody who lived in Poor Boy, and when he told them he was leaving town, they lost no time in wishing him a speedy journey. One of the storekeepers did not believe him when Spence said he was leaving town with his rent paid up and money in his pocket. "This is the first time I've ever heard of one of you Poor Boy people paying up your rent before skipping town," the storekeeper had said, winking at one of his other customers. "How did you manage that, Douthit?" Spence plunged his thumb at the storekeeper's ribs. "A good businessman can always get himself financed by knowing the right people," Spence told him. "It took me a while to find that out, though. I was on my uppers a heap of times before I caught on to how it's done, but now I know. Right this minute I'm as much on my feet as anybody in town." The storekeeper shook his head doubtfully. "I guess I'll wait till I hear the other side of the story before making up my mind," he had said.

Spence stopped in the middle of the street and studied

the house critically for several minutes. What worried him most, aside from having lost and spent the greater part of the money, was the fact that Mavis had run away again. Now that the time had come for them to leave, it made him feel more guilty than ever to be thinking of going away without Mavis. Maud's health was sufficient reason for leaving her behind, but he had no excuse for going home without Mavis after Miss Saunders had made him promise to take her.

He walked slowly across the yard towards the rear of the house wondering if he should make one final effort to get Mavis. He shook his head as he thought of going back to The White Turkey. He should have gone out there the night before, when he had plenty of money, if he went at all; besides, even if Mavis should agree to come with him, which she probably wouldn't do, there would not be enough money for two bus tickets.

By the time he reached the back steps, his mind was fully made up. Even if he could not think of a sound excuse for leaving Mavis behind, he could think of any number of good reasons why he should not change his own plans. He got down on his hands and knees and hid the bourbon and beer under the porch, covering the bottles with handfuls of sand and powdery white earth. Libby had been able to take care of herself in the city, he told himself, and if Libby had done it, he could think of no reason why Mavis could not do it, too. He crawled from under the porch and dusted off his pants. If Libby had given Maud a little money for food and tonic now and then, Mavis ought to do likewise. Spence felt a lot

186

better after that. He could leave Maud and Mavis behind now without a guilty conscience bothering him.

Maud was asleep on the pile of clothes in the corner when he went into the house. Now that he had made some changes in their plans he was sorry he had wasted three dollars on the alligator purse. Maud would not be able to use it, and the three dollars in cash would have done him a lot of good. Spence stood beside her, looking at the purse in his hand and wondering what he should do with it. Just when he had made up his mind to take it back to the store and ask for the return of the money, Maud opened her eyes and sat up. The first thing she noticed was the brown alligator purse, and before he could hide it behind his back, she had reached out and grabbed it. Spence could not keep from feeling sorry for her. She still believed she was going back to Beaseley County when he went.

"Now, that's real pretty, Spence," she said as she admired the purse. She held it at arm's length and gazed at it lovingly. After that she held it against her nose, closing her eyes while she smelled its peculiar odor. "It's just what I need to carry Dr. Munday's in while I ride to Beaseley County." Spence watched her grimly. "In all my life I aint never seen a prettier thing than this. It's just what I've craved for the longest time."

Spence reached down and picked up the sack of tonic. He turned the sack upside-down on the clothes-pile. Maud's eyes began to glow as three large-size bottles of tonic tumbled on the quilt.

"I figured you'd be needing some tonic, Maud," he

187

told her. "While I was about it, I went ahead and got three big ones for you."

"There aint never been anybody as thoughtful of a human's comfort as you, Spence," she said gratefully as she ran her fingers over the bottles, touching them affectionately. "There aint many men in the world who'd take the trouble to get three bottles of Dr. Munday's at once."

She held up one of the bottles, silently indicating that she wanted him to open it for her. Spence got the corkscrew from the hook behind the door and pulled the stopper. Maud turned up the bottle and drank a third of the tonic before stopping for breath. She looked up at him, licking her lips.

"You ought to go easy on the tonic, so it'll last longer, Maud," he told her, wondering how she was going to get tonic when he was no longer there. It made him feel sad to be going away and leaving her all alone. "It'd be a pity if you used it all up in one day. Just try to go easy on it so it'll spread out more." He took the partly-empty bottle and placed it on the floor against the wall. "Now, just lay there and think about it, Maud. Thinking about it will do just about as much good for a while."

Maud picked up the brown alligator purse and discovered that it had a long strap she could put over her shoulder. She was more pleased than ever when she found that out, and she slipped it over her head. That was no sooner done than she was stretching out her arm and wiggling her fingers at the tonic bottle against the wall. Spence gave it to her, and she drank half the tonic left in the bottle before putting it down. When he left the room, she was curled up on the pile of clothes with the purse held tightly against her stomach.

Spence crawled under the back porch and dug up a bottle of beer and a pint of bourbon. He opened both and, holding one in each hand, sat down in the shade. He knew he had a lot of things to do before he could leave, but the heat of the day made him tired, and he felt like resting after the hot tiresome walk from town. He took a drink of bourbon, a swallow of beer. Each time he tilted his head back to take a drink, he was certain he saw somebody watching him from the Mitchells' window.

He could think of many things he was determined to do before leaving and getting on the bus, but he could think of none at that particular moment that was more important than getting even with Chet Mitchell. He tilted back his head and took another drink from each of the bottles, being careful this time to find out whether it was Chet or Myrt who was watching him. The curtains moved, and he got a glimpse of Myrt. She had taken off her clothes as usual at that time of afternoon, and he could see her in the window as plainly as he would have if she had been standing on the porch. He held up the bourbon bottle and measured the amount that was left. The beer was gone, and he tossed the empty bottle across the yard. From the corners of his eyes he could see Myrt lean out the window and watch the empty beer bottle roll out of sight in the weeds.

After waiting a while to find out what Myrt was going to do next, as he was certain she could not for long resist the urge to ask him for a drink, he crawled under the porch and got two more bottles. Bringing them out, he dusted them carefully and strolled to the edge of his yard. Myrt immediately ran to another window where she could see him better.

"Where's Chet?" he called to her.

She made no reply, but he could see her standing behind the curtains.

"Is Chet home?" he called a little more loudly. "If he aint, I've got something for you, Myrt. If he is, tell him to go to hell."

She parted the curtains and looked out the window. He could see her gazing wistfully at the bourbon and beer.

"Who's all that for, Spence?" she asked.

"Who you reckon?" he said teasingly.

"Now you stop that, Spence Douthit!" she said with impatience. "Tell me what you're going to do with it!"

"I aint going to waste it, for one thing. It's too hard to come by."

"It's been a long time since I had some."

"That's what you get for marrying a stingy-minded husband."

He strolled to the Mitchells' porch and put the bottles down.

"I wouldn't be against sharing it with the right party," Spence said. "But that don't mean with Chet."

"Chet's gone off somewhere," she said at once.

"When's he coming home?"

"No time soon, that I know about."

190

Spence picked up the bottles and went to the steps. Myrt disappeared from the window, but in a few moments she was standing just inside the kitchen door. He could see her holding up a finger and motioning to him with it.

"You aint fooling me, are you, Myrt?" he asked suspiciously. "Chet aint hid somewhere in the house just waiting for me to put my foot inside?"

"I'm telling the truth, Spence. Why don't you come on in out of the sun?"

Spence saw her backing away from the door. He looked around behind him before stepping up to the porch.

"I aint so sure," he said when he got to the screendoor. He pressed his face against the dusty screen and peered into the kitchen. He could see Myrt beckoning to him. "An old dog like me always takes care not to get his tail caught in a trap."

"Aw, come on, Spence," she said impatiently. "Don't be scared. There's nobody else here."

He opened the screendoor, thrust his head into the kitchen, and looked it over carefully. Myrt had gone as far as the door leading into the bedroom, and she was once more beckoning to him with her finger.

"If I get trapped this time," Spence said aloud, "I'll sure-God know better next time."

He stepped into the kitchen, closing the door softly behind him, and listened intently for a moment before going into the next room with Myrt.

When he got there, Myrt ran to the bed and sat down. Spence looked the room over carefully, afterward getting

191

down on his hands and knees and looking under the bed. When he got up, Myrt was waiting, and he sat down beside her.

"Open them up, Spence," she urged, pointing at the bottles in his hands.

He pulled the stopper from the bourbon bottle and handed it to her. While he was prying off the beer bottle cap with his teeth, Myrt took a long noisy drink. She wiped her mouth with the back of her hand and put the bottle back into his hand. He offered her a drink of beer, but she shook her head. Spence took a mouthful of bourbon and followed it with a long drink of beer.

"I wouldn't even study about being here if I wasn't getting ready to leave for good," he told her in a diffident manner. "I don't believe in fooling around with neighbor-women. I know too many ways for things to go wrong."

Myrt took another drink of bourbon, making a wry face after swallowing the liquor, and reached for the beer. Spence leaned back on his elbow and watched her with an appraising eye while she drank. Myrt was large, and inclined to be stout, but at that moment he could find no other fault with her appearance.

"It does an old rascal like me good to see a fine healthy-looking woman for a change," he told her. "I've got so used to looking at Maud and her measly self that I'd just about forgotten what the other kind look like."

"Now, you stop teasing me, Spence," she said, giggling a little. "I know I aint no flaming beauty."

"Maybe you aint no flaming beauty," he agreed, "but

192

you sure can give some woman a lot to lose sleep worrying about. Why, just look at that there! Now that's something! If you'd seen all the skinny women I have in my time, you'd appreciate the way you show up before a man. A woman like you can give an ordinary man an awful lot of comfort."

"You're just teasing me," she said, slapping at him. Spence ducked his head to dodge her hand. She leaned over and grabbed him by the ear. "Now, you quit it, Spence!" she said, twisting his ear.

"You quit it yourself!" he said as he pushed at her. She held on to his ear until he tickled her under the arms. Then she burst into giggles and rolled over on her back.

Spence took another stiff drink of bourbon, following it with a swallow of the warm beer.

"I wouldn't be here if it wasn't because I'm fixing to leave town for good," he told her. He leaned back on his elbows and resumed his appraisal of her. "I wouldn't be here for anything if I wasn't moving off. I said to myself I'd come over here when Chet wasn't around and let you know about it. Of course, I aint got a thing on my mind aside from that. It's just a friendly, neighborly, social visit. I wouldn't want to come over here with my mind all loaded down beforehand."

"I don't know what you're talking about," Myrt said coyly. "I don't know what you mean."

"And I sure-God wouldn't be here if Chet was around. Dogbite it if he aint the contrariest man in the whole world. I've seen him come out on his back porch, lean out as far as he could get, and empty his slop-jar spang in my back yard, and then on top of all that, stand there and laugh his fool head off about it. It takes a real mean man to do a contrary thing like that to a neighbor."

"Somebody stole all the pullets we had in our chicken house," Myrt said. "It takes a real mean man to steal a neighbor's pullets, too."

Spence sat up, compressing his lips and glaring at her angrily.

"There wasn't no excuse for raking that up!" he said in a loud voice. "That happened 'way in the past."

"So's everything else, so far," she said, laughing.

Spence gave her a shove and pushed her down upon the bed. Myrt tried to reach one of his ears but he got up before she could get her hand on him. His feet knocked over the empty bourbon bottle.

"I don't take no back-talk from my women," he told her sternly. "Now, if you're going to drink my liquor and try to back-talk me, I'm leaving."

Myrt sat up and waited meekly for him to scold her.

"You'd better make up your mind before you ask for another drop of my bourbon," he said, shaking his head with quick motions.

"Aw, now, Spence," she said soothingly. "Let's don't me and you fight about nothing."

He sat down on the side of the bed and put his arms around her. "You must've had me figured out all wrong," he told her crossly. "I'm a real he-man when my tail's up."

"You'd better be careful," she warned him. "Chet might be coming home. If he caught you——"

"To hell with Chet!" Spence said. He hugged her until she couldn't get her breath. "Chet can go somewhere else to do his bird-dogging! When I get my tail up, I do my own pointing!"

Myrt managed to get a tight grip on his ear. He tried to push her away, but Myrt held her grip. Spence tried once more to tickle her under the arms, but this time nothing happened. His ear felt as if it would be torn from his head any second.

"Let go!" he yelled at her.

He drew back his fist to hit her when the sound of an automobile coming up the street made them both stop and listen. Myrt released his ear, and Spence stood up and craned his neck to see out the window. As the sound of the car grew louder, both ran to the window to see who was coming. The small black sedan stopped in front of Spence's house, and a moment later Miss Saunders stepped out. She waited for a while as if expecting somebody to come out and meet her, and then walked cautiously down the path towards the front door.

"Who's that?" Myrt asked beside him.

"It's Miss Saunders," he told her. "She's looking for me."

Myrt locked her arms around him.

"You stay here with me, Spence," she begged. "Don't pay no attention to her. I'll give you a better time than she can."

He struggled free and ran to the back door. Myrt caught him before he could reach the porch.

"I've got to get there before Maud sees her," he told

Myrt excitedly. "Maud's liable to lose her temper, and somebody might get hurt. I can't let that happen."

"But what about me?" Myrt asked in a hurt tone. "What about me, Spence?"

Spence looked around at her.

"If I can get through with her in time, I'll be back," he promised.

Myrt threw her arms around him, pinning his arms helplessly at his sides. When she tried to pull him back into the house, he raised his knee and hit her with it as hard as he could. Myrt doubled up, wrapping her arms around her stomach. Spence dashed for home.

When he reached his own back yard, he looked back over his shoulder and saw Myrt coming after him. She was staggering a little, but she managed to keep on in his direction. Hoping to leave her behind, he ran around the corner of his house; but when he leaped up on the front porch and ran to the door, Myrt was still coming. Spence ran past Miss Saunders, who was looking at Maud on the pile of old clothes, and almost knocked her down in his haste to get on the other side of her. When he stopped, completely out of breath, and looked to see what had happened to Myrt, she was standing at the door.

CHAPTER FOURTEEN

MISS SAUNDERS, SEEING MYRT AT THE
door, held her breath as long as she could; then, with an
unexpectedness that startled everyone, she shrieked at the
top of her voice. Spence jumped as if he had been scared
out of his wits, and even Miss Saunders herself, frightened by her own cry, began to shake and tremble.

The piercing scream woke up Maud, who took one
swift look at the room and leaped to the floor. Her un-
combed graying hair was hanging in knotted strings over
her face like the tousled fringe on a shawl, and she tried
to sweep it from her eyes with one hand while clutching
at the slipping nightgown with the other.

By that time Miss Saunders' voice had come back to
her, and she hastily looked from one face to another.

"What in the world!" she cried, looking at Myrt and
quickly clapping her hands on her face. "I've never been
so shocked in my life!"

"Miss," Spence said shakily as he tried to watch all

three of the women at the same time, "don't get upset. Myrt didn't mean to jar you like that."

Maud, hitting at the strings of hair hanging over her eyes, glared first at one woman and then at the other as though she could not decide which one to leap upon first. At last she stopped looking at Miss Saunders and ran to the middle of the room.

"Maud, don't go and get all feathered-out," Spence pleaded when he realized what she was about to do.

She ignored Spence completely, not even bothering to speak to him. Myrt, seeing Maud move closer, hastily backed to the porch. Maud ran to the door.

"You'd better get away from my house, Myrt Mitchell!" Maud yelled. "If I ever got my hands on you, I'd pull every hair out of that scurvy head of yours. If I could find a stick, I'd grab it and beat the daylights out of you."

Myrt turned and ran for home as fast as she could. Maud stood on the porch watching her until the Mitchells' screendoor slammed before coming back into the room. Spence stepped aside out of her way when she trotted past him. Miss Saunders was nervous and trembling.

"Now, Maudie—" Spence said soothingly.

She stopped midway between him and Miss Saunders.

"Spence Douthit, if you dare bring any more sporting women to this house, I'll—I'll——"

"But, now, Maudie——"

"Shut your mouth! You aint going to Maudie me out of me speaking my mind!"

She paused, took a deep breath, and fixed her gaze

198

upon Miss Saunders, regarding her as though she had been overlooked until that moment. Miss Saunders, who was already pale with fear, became more perturbed with each painful throb of her heart. She glanced nervously at the door, but Maud took several steps forward, effectively blocking her only means of escape.

"Maudie, let me explain things to you," Spence said nervously.

A wave of Maud's hand silenced him.

"Who're you?" Maud demanded hoarsely of Miss Saunders. "Aint you that female who——"

"That's Miss Saunders, Maud," Spence spoke up. "She's the kind lady who's been coming here to help us out. Now, don't go and spoil things by getting mad again, because we want her to go ahead and do what she wants to do for us. If it wasn't for her, we'd be in a sorry fix. It's a pity there aint more like her in the world."

"Now, aint that nice?" Maud said sarcastically. She twisted her face into a scowl. "Why don't you go about your business somewhere else!"

"Now, please, Mrs. Douthit," Miss Saunders began anxiously, "please let me explain!" She put her hands behind her back and felt blindly for the wall. "None of the things you suspect are true. I am a respectable woman, I'll have you know. I've been coming here because it is my duty. I don't know what you've said about me behind my back, but you certainly owe me an apology for some of the things you've said in my presence. In our work we social workers maintain a strictly impersonal attitude. You might say that social workers are sexless."

"I might say it, sister, but I won't!" Maud said contemptuously. She looked Miss Saunders up and down. "I don't know who you think you're fooling, sister, but it aint me."

Miss Saunders caught her breath sharply and held it as long as she could.

"This case was assigned to me by Mrs. Jouett and I intend doing my best regardless of the insults I have to take. Mrs. Jouett expects me to——"

"I'm the one who does the expecting and everything else, too, around here," Maud stated flatly. "I don't appreciate nobody butting in my private life. I've lived long enough to know that if there's a man around, you women aint got a bit of shame about nosing him out. The last time I caught you here, I told you I'd kill you if you came sporting around here again. I meant it when I said it, and I still mean it!"

Maud looked around the room for something to hit her with. There was not a stick of furniture left in the house, but she saw the empty tonic bottle against the wall. Keeping her eyes on Miss Saunders, she backed towards the bottle. Miss Saunders looked appealingly at Spence and, when she saw he was making no attempt to protect her from his wife, she edged cautiously towards the door. Just as Maud put her hand on the bottle, Miss Saunders screamed and dashed from the house. She reached the porch safely, but Maud ran after her, swinging the bottle threateningly. Spence went out the back door and sprinted to the front yard.

When he got in front of the house, Miss Saunders was

half-way to the street and Maud was poised on the steps.

"I'll kill her!" Maud yelled. "So help me God, I'll beat the brains out of her!" she cried. Spence glanced down the street. He could see the neighbors running out on their front porches to find out what the commotion was about. Some of them walked part way up the street in order to get a better view. "I've seen the likes of her before, and I aint too big a fool not to know a sporting woman when I set eyes on one. If she don't get her nasty self away from here, I'll kill her and be glad of it!"

Maud drew back her arm, pausing while she closed one eye and took careful aim, and then with all her might hurled the tonic bottle at Miss Saunders. Miss Saunders shut her eyes and, with her hands over her face, ran towards her car. The bottle missed her by a few feet, but it struck the rear fender on the sedan and crashed to pieces. Splinters of broken glass showered dangerously upon her. The neighbors came closer to see what was going to happen next. Maud searched the porch frantically for something else to hurl at Miss Saunders, but she was unable to find anything at all. However, she went to the steps and stuck out her tongue. Miss Saunders ducked behind the automobile for protection in case Maud found something else to throw at her.

One of the neighbors, who had come closer than any of the others, called down the street to somebody. "These Douthits are at it again, Jim!" he said in a loud voice. Spence waved his arms at the man and urged him to go away and leave them alone. The man went back down the street laughing to himself.

Miss Saunders peeped around the back of the car to see what Maud was doing.

"I'm warning you for the last time to stay away from here!" Maud yelled with renewed vigor. She made an ugly face at Miss Saunders, sticking out her tongue. "This is the last time I'm warning you, too! The next time I catch you here, I'll slap those fluffy tits clear to the other side of that canal. You sporting females aint got the shame of a bung-hole in a barrel!"

Spence waited tensely at the corner of the yard. He watched Miss Saunders, but at the same time took care to keep a safe distance between him and Maud. He could see Miss Saunders crouching on the ground behind her car. She was peeping around the fender at him.

Maud thrust her head forward, at the same time sticking out her tongue as far as she could and wiggling it at Miss Saunders. Miss Saunders took one look and ducked out of sight. After several moments Maud pulled up her nightgown and strode into the house, slamming the screendoor behind her with all her might. Most of the neighbors went back into their houses after that.

Spence waited until he was sure Maud was not coming back. Then, crouching over as far as he could, he ran to the car. He found Miss Saunders squatting on the ground and trembling with fright.

"Miss, it looks like everything in God's world's gone wrong," he told her apologetically. "I just don't know what gets into Maud when she has one of them spells. She just can't hold her tongue at a time like that. And it looks like it gets worse all the time, because it sure-God aint getting no better."

Miss Saunders, appearing small and childlike in her cramped position, looked up at him. Her eyes were large and round, and she was gripping her fists in an effort to control herself. He had never seen her look so helpless before.

"What have I done to make your wife distrust me so, Mr. Douthit? What could I have done?"

"You aint done a thing wrong, Miss. It's just Maud's devilish nature to go on a wild rampage like that when she's upset. It wouldn't have happened this time if I'd known you was coming, because I'd been out here to head you off before you went in the house."

"Who was that other woman—the one with no clothes on? What was she doing——"

"Oh, that was just a neighbor-woman, Miss. She just happens to live next door."

"What was she doing running around like that?"

"You know how womenfolks is sometimes, Miss. One'll get a notion in her head about something or other, and then they don't stop at nothing. Myrt's a sensible creature most of the time, however, and that's the only time she ever came to my front door like that. Generally, she stays out back."

Miss Saunders stood up. She brushed the wrinkles from her skirt and patted her hair.

"Well," she said sternly. "I don't approve of it, no matter where she stays. It's just not decent."

Spence nodded because he knew she expected him to

agree with her. Miss Saunders was regarding him coldly.

"Mr. Douthit," she asked sharply, "why didn't you leave on the bus this morning?"

"I was just fixing to explain about that, Miss."

"I waited there two hours for you to come. I had a basket lunch all put up and ready for you. Then you never came. Why didn't you? What happened?"

"Miss, it was like this. I was ready to——"

"Did you buy the bus tickets with the money I gave you?" she interrupted.

"I was just fixing to explain about that, Miss. Last night when I——"

"Where's Mavis?" she asked impatiently. "I didn't see her when I was in the house a few minutes ago. Where is Mavis, Mr. Douthit?"

Spence looked at the house as though he expected to see Mavis standing on the porch.

"Mavis?" he repeated to himself. "Oh, she's around somewhere." He watched Miss Saunders from the corners of his eyes. "I reckon she just stepped out for a while."

"I don't believe it!" she snapped. "I can't believe anything you say any more." He watched her twisting her fingers nervously. "You're not telling me the truth!"

"Now, Miss, I—" he began defensively.

"When are you leaving?" she demanded coldly, staring him in the eyes.

"Almost anytime now," he assured her. "I aint going to lose a speck of time once I get started. I aim to get going as soon as I can."

"Do you still have the thirty dollars I gave you?"

"Well, maybe not every last penny of it."

"You mean you've spent some of that money?"

"You know how money gets away sometimes, Miss."

"How much do you have left?"

"You mean exactly how much?"

"You know what I mean!" she cried. "Do you have twenty dollars, or twenty-five, or what?"

"I hate to disappoint you, Miss, but I reckon there's only three or four of it left." He dropped his head until his chin rested upon his chest. "Somehow the money just went, like money always does," he said guiltily. "It went before I knew it, Miss."

Miss Saunders gasped. She held her breath for second after second while Spence averted his eyes. Finally he heard her sigh.

"You make me so angry I could just—just—I don't know what!" he heard her say. She remained silent after that until he looked up at her from beneath his brows. "This is terrible!" she exclaimed. "How in the world will I ever be able to explain this to Mrs. Jouett? I should have known better than to give you that money in the first place, and I was a fool for listening to you. I believed I could trust you to buy the tickets and leave town, and you took advantage of me. You never intended going to the bus station this morning. All you wanted was to get your hands on that money so you could throw it away. If Mrs. Jouett finds out about this, she'll never forgive me. And if she doesn't dismiss me, I'll be the laughing-stock of the Welfare Department. I've trained myself so thoroughly for this type of work, too. All my life I've looked forward to the time when I could devote myself to helping others, and it's so cruel to make me suffer such humiliation. I'll never get over it. And if I am dismissed, Mrs. Jouett would never give me a letter of recommendation, either! What will I do! What's to become of my career!"

Spence watched her solemnly. He tried to think of something to say that would make her feel better, but nothing that came to mind seemed appropriate at the moment.

"After all I've tried to do for you, I can't bear to have you do this to me!" she cried. "My career will be completely ruined."

"I'll try to do what I can, Miss," Spence said. "I'll go out and find me a little job somewhere and make a big thing of it. In time, I'll be able to pay you back."

"What good would that do?" she said angrily. "Once dismissed from the Welfare Department, I'll never be reinstated."

Spence cringed.

"And Mavis isn't here, either," she stated accusingly. "You've spent the bus fare on yourself and not even bothered to get your daughter." She suddenly bent forward, sniffing suspiciously. "You spent that money for liquor! I can smell it on you! You reek with it!"

Spence drew in his breath. "Well, there aint no use in telling a lie about that," he admitted. "I did buy me a little."

He could see tears forming in her eyes as she stared at

him. Soon the tears were trickling down her cheeks. She made no attempt to hide them.

"You—you—you are impossible!" she cried.

Her eyes blinked several times and she rubbed them with the knuckles of her hands.

"You make me so mad I could just shake you!" she said. "If I were a man, I'd—I'd hit you!"

Spence took a step backward.

"The worst thing about it all is that Mrs. Jouett will find out what happened after the warning she gave me. She trusted me so, too! I promised her you'd cooperate with us, and now what will she say? What will she say!"

"If that's that horse-faced woman who came stomping around here, it aint going to bother me one little bit," Spence spoke up unhesitatingly.

"Oh, shut up!" Miss Saunders cried.

"Now, Miss, let me explain——"

"Doggone you!"

Spence's mouth fell agape. He could see her gritting her teeth while her lips opened and closed with twitching motions.

"You talk exactly like some of the folks back home in Beaseley County," he said, still surprised by what she had called him. "Some folks up there used to get so provoked at Maud and me that they'd call us the same thing just like you did. They called us the doggone Douthits. It makes me downright homesick to hear it said. There's another family of Douthits living up there, sort of second or third cousins of mine 'way back, and people call them just Douthits. But most everybody in Beaseley County calls me and my folks the doggone Douthits. It's queer how you thought of saying the same thing."

"I don't blame them at all for calling you that," she said. "Because that's exactly what you are!"

"And even down here there are folks who say the same thing now and then," Spence continued. "Not all of them say it because they're mad at me, but just because they like to say it. It seems to fit, somehow."

"It certainly does fit!" she said. "I'm surprised that I didn't think of it sooner!"

She leaned against the car and gazed down the street. Spence waited. He knew she was thinking about something, but he had no idea what was occupying her mind. After a while, when some of her anger had disappeared, she turned around.

"How much money did you say you have left?" she asked impersonally. "And remember to tell me the truth!"

"Three or four dollars," he replied meekly.

"Is that all!"

"It's lucky I've got that much left, Miss. When I started spending it, I thought of a heap of things Maud and me needed bad."

"Oh, darn!" Miss Saunders said with impatience.

"But if I had it back, I'd do the right thing with it," he assured her.

"I wish I could depend on that."

"You sure could, Miss, if you wanted to chance it."

Miss Saunders laughed to herself.

"What am I going to do with you?" she asked, turning her head a little to one side and studying his face closely.

"What could I possibly do with a man like you? I can't trust you, I can't force you to leave, and my pleading has no effect on you. It's all so hopeless!"

"If you'd give me another chance, Miss," he said with a serious tone, "I'll do just like you say. I try hard, but when my shortcomings catch up with me, I somehow don't have the nerve to fight them off. This time, though, I'll promise to leave town."

"But you promised last time, too."

"I know, but this time I'll cross my heart and hope to die, Miss. Last time I forgot to do that, and I reckon that's why it didn't hold up."

Miss Saunders nodded to herself as she quickly made up her mind to try once more. She opened her pocket-book and took out several greenbacks. Spence's eyes widened hopefully when he saw the money.

"I can't give you a penny more of the Welfare Department funds," she said, "but I'm going to give you some of my own money." She counted the bills and frowned at him. "This is all I have until I receive my next pay, but I'm going to give it to you—if you'll promise faithfully to leave town."

"I sure-God wouldn't hesitate to say a little thing like that, Miss," he was quick to tell her.

He reached for the money in her hand, but she held it behind her back out of his reach.

"There's one more thing you'll have to promise me before I'll give it to you."

"I wouldn't hesitate to promise that, neither."

"Promise me you'll never tell a soul that I gave you

twenty dollars of my own money after you'd spent the Welfare Department's thirty dollars."

"Dogbite my pecker if that aint the easiest promise I ever made, Miss!"

She drew her hand from behind her back, held it at her side indecisively for a moment, and then, accompanied by a deep sigh, flung her partly closed fist at him. Spence bent over eagerly and with thumb and forefinger extracted the bills. Miss Saunders bit her lips as she saw him stuff the money into his watch-pocket.

"Now, please, get out of town, Mr. Douthit!" she begged without shame. "Please go right away before something else dreadful happens! Please, for my sake, Mr. Douthit!"

Spence backed away, muttering assurances with every step. He was anxious to get beyond her reach before she could change her mind and demand the return of her money. She stood beside her car, a doubtful frown covering her face, as he hurried towards the house.

"You doggone Douthits!" she cried as tears blinded her. She wiped her eyes and jerked open the car door. "You doggone Douthits, you!"

CHAPTER FIFTEEN

A HUGE BLACK CLOUD, SWEEPING INLAND
from the Gulf, was rapidly darkening the earth. As the
wind roared up the canal, children ran for home and
small whirlwinds dipped into the street, sucking up dust
and scraps of paper. Spence went to the porch just as a
gust of wind wrenched loose a sheet of rusty tin roofing
and sent it crashing against the side of the Mitchells'
house. Rain began falling in large round drops and, with
a blinding flash, a streak of lightning blazed over the
town. A moment afterward came the explosive crack of
thunder. Spence ran into the house. Already torrents of
water were beating upon the roof, and streams were running down the walls and pouring from the ceiling. Maud
pulled the quilt over her head and held her hands against
her ears to escape the sounds of the wind and thunder.

The thunderstorm passed over, but the sky remained
dark and sunless. Spence went to the back porch and
looked at the sheets of rainwater covering the yard and

the weed-grown vacant lots beside the canal. Frogs were croaking on the canal banks, and night was not far away. He decided it was too late to do anything about leaving that day; tomorrow would be just as good for starting the trip as any other time. He shivered in the unaccustomed coolness and stepped carefully over the pool of rainwater at the bottom of the stoop. The bourbon and beer were still in the hiding place when he crawled under the porch, but the bottles were muddy and he had to wash them in rainwater before he could open them. After that he sat down on the edge of the porch and took several drinks. Maud called him, and he hastily put the bottles under the step and went inside.

"I want you to go out there and speak your mind, Spence," she told him as soon as he walked into the room. "I don't want you to be backward about it, neither."

"What in the world are you talking about?" he asked bewilderedly.

She got up, took him firmly by the arm, and led him to the front door. "I want you to put a stop to that," she said with a meaningful shake of her head.

A large moving truck was backing up to the front porch. Spence stepped through the door as Maud shoved him forward.

"I don't know who it is and I don't care what they want," she said, "but you're going out there and put an end to whatever it is. Now, get out there and stop it!"

The heavy moving truck gave a final lurch as the tires chewed into the loose wet sand and backed against the porch. The house groaned and creaked as the timbers rocked on the foundation. The rear end of the truck crunched into the pine flooring, and several boards buckled and splintered.

"Don't stand there like a plain fool!" Maud yelled. "Do something!"

The driver jumped to the ground and came splashing through the standing rainwater to the rear of the truck. With a single flourish of his arm he unfastened the gate of the truck body. A pile of furniture, boxes, bundles, and a crate of white rabbits tumbled to the porch. Spence jumped backward as the rabbit crate rolled towards him. When it came to a stop, he bent over and stared confusedly at the mass of pink round eyes and twitching noses.

Maud kicked him with all her might in the seat of his pants.

"Do something, you durn fool!" she yelled. "Stop that crowd!"

He looked up and saw a heavy-set man of about forty-five who was dressed in faded overalls. He was wearing a ragged-edged field-straw hat, the kind Spence had always worn in Beaseley County in summer. The man paid no attention to Spence. The large blonde-haired woman with him was holding a sheet of kitchen oilcloth over her head to protect her from the few scattered raindrops that fell from time to time. The man and his wife came sliding out of the truck to the porch, and right behind them came half-a-dozen towheaded children of all sizes who lost no time in scrambling to their feet and jumping up and down on the boxes and bundles.

"Now, just hold on here, who ever you folks are!" Spence said determinedly. "You folks must be at the wrong place. This here is where I live."

Three of the younger children were standing in a semicircle before Spence and gaping at him as if they had never seen a human being before in their lives. Spence tried to shoo them away, but they paid no attention to him. The oldest girl, who appeared to be about fifteen, and who stood off at a distance, averted her eyes each time he looked at her. A boy of ten took charge of the rabbits by standing the crate on its end and jostling the animals into a squirming mass of white fur. All the children, with the exception of the older girl, were barefooted and dirty-faced. The girl wore high-heeled pumps and short yellow socks.

"You people just hold on, now," Spence spoke up authoritatively. "Don't nobody take another step!"

The driver, who had been flinging pieces of household goods from the truck, stopped and walked over to Spence.

"This is 720 South Maybank, aint it?" he demanded surlily, at the same time pointing at the rusty tin numerals over the door. "It's 720, aint it, pappy?"

"That's right, but——"

"Then what're you bellyaching about, pappy?"

"Something's gone wrong somewhere," Spence insisted, "because this here place——"

"What about it?" the driver said impatiently.

"Well, because these people aint got no right to be moving in here like this."

214

"You'd better talk to the big fellow over there in the overalls, pappy. I don't get paid for listening."

Two of the children made a dash for the front door, and as they ducked past Maud she slapped at them. Another pair, seeing Maud slapping at the others, jumped off the porch and ran around to the rear of the house.

"Jessica," the mother called, "hurry and help get these things inside so we can start supper."

The girl's eyes met Spence's gaze, but she quickly looked in another direction. He forgot all about stopping the family from moving into the house while he watched her stoop over and pick up some of the bundles. The truck driver pulled at Spence's sleeve.

"Pappy, you'd better get your satisfaction out of the big fellow over there," he told Spence, "or I'm going ahead and unload. I can't hang around here all night."

Spence stepped over the crate of rabbits and walked up to the man in overalls.

"Maybe it aint none of my business," Spence said, "but it does make me kind of curious to know what you're doing moving all your stuff in here like this."

"I'm Tom Claiborne," the man said with a hearty smile. He was good-natured and friendly, and Spence found himself shaking Claiborne's out-stretched hand. "Me and my family's moved in to live here," he said with a chuckle.

"That's what it looks like to me, too," Spence said as he continued shaking the stranger's hand. "However, you've sort of got things mixed up somewhere." Spence

215

succeeded in freeing his hand from Claiborne's grip. "This is where me and my family live, and there aint enough room for mine and yours both, especially with that pack of young ones thrown in to boot."

"I paid a month's rent in advance on this place today," Claiborne said proudly. "If that don't make a man feel at home, I sure don't know what does."

Claiborne picked up several heavy boxes and moved towards the door. With several days' growth of wiry black beard covering his face and neck he looked awesome and unreasonable, and Spence promptly stepped out of his way. When he got to the door, he stopped with a courteous nod of his head and allowed Maud sufficient time to get out of his way if she chose to do so; Maud did not move an inch, so Claiborne bowed with a short nod and walked into the house. Maud was pushed back into the room.

While Claiborne was dropping the boxes in the middle of the floor, Maud was running to the pile of clothes in the corner. She sat down with a possessive air.

"There aint nobody going to drive me out of here!" she stated in a defiant manner. "I know my rights!"

Mrs. Claiborne and Jessica walked through the room on their way to the kitchen with boxes of food and cooking utensils. Maud made an ugly face and stuck out her tongue.

"I'll sit right here till I'm dead, before I'll let anybody come here and order me around," she told Claiborne.

"You aint bothering us a bit if you want to squat there in the corner, ma'am. We aint been figuring on using that corner, anyway. You're welcome to it just as long as you don't die in it."

Two of the children raced through the room, leaping over boxes and dodging their father. They passed close to Maud. Even though they were beyond her reach, she nonetheless made a wide sweeping swing at their heads with her open hand.

"I'll slap those brats silly yet!" Maud shouted.

"If there's slapping to be done around here, ma'am, I'll do it myself," Claiborne told her.

When Claiborne went to the porch to carry the beds inside, Spence watched him until they were set up in the two rooms. Then he walked through the house towards the kitchen. Jessica had made a fire in the stove, and Mrs. Claiborne put a pan of beans on to boil. Spence watched the preparations for supper as long as he could, and then walked up and down the porch wondering how he was going to get some of the food for himself. The odors coming from the kitchen were more than he could endure without trying to get something to eat, and so he went back to the kitchen and sat down at the table. Mrs. Claiborne glanced at him, but he could find no encouragement in her manner. Jessica watched him shyly.

"Looks like we're going to be a little cramped for space, all staying in the same house with so few beds to go around," he said as he watched Mrs. Claiborne. He waited for her to make some comment, but she went about getting supper ready as though she had not heard him. "My wife's satisfied with what she's got for a place to sleep," he told them, "but I've got myself to look out for. I never was comfortable on anything short of a bed."

Mrs. Claiborne continued to ignore him, and Spence leaned back and waited. Jessica set the table and placed a gallon jug of black molasses in the center of it. Spence leaned forward and wiped his finger around the rim of the jug's mouth. He sucked his finger, smacking his lips noisily. Presently Mrs. Claiborne brought a pan of cornbread to the table, and Spence helped himself to a large slice. He poured a cupful of the black molasses and got ready to eat. Tom Claiborne came in and sat down at the opposite end of the table.

"What's your name?" Claiborne asked him.

"Spence Douthit," he replied, stuffing the cornbread into his mouth. He chewed hungrily as he watched Claiborne across the table. "If you've lived in this part of the world any time at all, you might've heard of me. Nearly everybody else around here has at some time or another."

"I aint lived here before, and I never heard of you," Claiborne said. His wife brought a dish of steaming hot beans and put it in front of Claiborne. He helped himself to the beans and cornbread. The children were continually running into the kitchen, snatching a hunk of cornbread from the table, and dashing out again. Spence ate as fast as he could, trying to fill his stomach before all the food was gone.

"Where'd you come from?" Spence asked him.

"Tennessee."

"Been down here long?"

"Two days."

"Two days?"

'That's right."

"What did you come for?"

"Looking for work."

"There's no jobs around here. You're in a bad fix."

"Couldn't be no worse than where I came from. There was no jobs there, either."

Spence pushed his plate away and wiped his mouth.

"If you don't watch out, you'll end up stranded just like me," he told Claiborne.

"I aint worrying," Claiborne said with a laugh. "I've already got my eye on a job."

"What kind?"

"Working for the city."

"How long's a job like that going to last?"

"Last?" Claiborne said. "There aint no end to it that I know about. It ought to last as long as me or the city lasts."

"You sure got a lot of confidence in things," Spence said with a shake of his head. "I used to be that way, too, when I had a job over at the powder plant. But it didn't take me long to stop talking so big when things started going wrong. If I was you, I'd take care. Jobs down here just seem to peter out when you're least expecting it. If you want to make use of good sense, you'll pick up and go back home while you can."

"I aint worrying," Claiborne laughed.

"I've heard a lot smarter men than me or you say exactly that same thing," Spence said, "and if you asked me to point them out to you, I'd have to dig right down to the bottom of the pile to show you. They're as down

219

and out as a human can get and still walk on two legs."

"That might be true about some people, but it aint about me. I can make a living here, yonder, or 'way to hell and gone. I aint worrying at all."

"You will be when those girls of yours start running wild down here," Spence said knowingly. "That's when you'll wish you'd paid me some mind."

Claiborne laughed and leaned back in his chair. He locked his hands behind his head and watched Spence with an amused smile on his face.

"And another thing," Spence said. "Anybody who moves to Poor Boy's on the first step going down. I was just as cocky as you when I first moved here. Now, I got better sense than to do it again. But you aint!"

He noticed that Claiborne was looking at the door. Spence turned around and saw Floyd Sharp.

"You got company, aint you, Spence?" Floyd said. "I didn't know you had company visiting you."

Spence got up and took Floyd to the back porch.

"It's just a mix-up, Floyd," he explained casually. "It'll all be straightened out by morning."

They sat down on the steps in the dark. Both were silent for a long time.

"Spence," Floyd said in a husky whisper.

"What?"

"I've got to tell you something, Spence."

"Go ahead, Floyd. You know you can trust me."

Spence waited as long as he could. Floyd was looking off into the darkness of the night.

"You think somebody knows about it, Floyd—somebody besides me?"

"It aint that," Floyd answered. "It's something else."

"What?"

"A little while ago I sort of lost my head, Spence," he began, speaking slowly. "Just after dark I got a notion that I ought to set fire to every house in Poor Boy and burn them down. I went over to the house next door to mine and started a fire under the back porch. Then I ran out in the weeds and hid. As soon as the people found out the house was on fire, they ran out and began pouring water on it and trying to put it out. The woman, Mrs. Williams, began crying, and then all the children began to bawl. I could hear everything they said where I was, and when I heard them crying because their house was burning up, I couldn't stand it any longer. I ran and stomped on the fire and helped pour water on it till it was out. I just couldn't stand to see poor people like Mrs. Williams lose her house and all they had. That's why I put the fire out. After that I couldn't make myself set fire to any more houses. It just wasn't right, Spence."

There was silence on the porch for several minutes. Spence could see Floyd looking at the glow of light reflected against the clouds over the city.

"I'm sure glad you didn't set fire to this house, Floyd," he said sighing with relief. "It aint much, but it's the only place Maud and me's got to stay in until we leave."

Floyd nodded but made no comment.

"I wouldn't worry about that no more, Floyd," Spence

said. "The house didn't burn down." He slapped Floyd on the knee. "You go on home and get some sleep."

"No," Floyd said firmly. "I can't do that. I couldn't sleep if I tried to. I've got to do something about those children of mine."

"What can you do, Floyd? You started out to burn down Poor Boy, but changed your mind. What else is there to do?"

"There's only one thing, Spence," he said. "That's for me to go and tell the police about Bubber. If I tell about that, it's the best chance I'll ever have to say why I done it. I've got it all figured out now. It's bound to work. I aint just jumping in the dark. Somebody will listen to me. Somebody will understand why I had to kill him. I just couldn't keep on living and seeing my girls grow up in Poor Boy. I know what I'm doing. They'll send me away for a while, but they'll put my girls in a home and take care of them. It's the proper thing to do, Spence. If I hadn't killed Bubber, I wouldn't be so quick to try to do something that'll help my girls. Now I've got a good reason. I just couldn't bear to take all those little girls over to the canal and drown them like I talked about doing. That wouldn't be right, Spence. It just wouldn't be right."

"All that makes me feel guilty for ever bringing that Bubber down here in the first place," Spence said. "If I hadn't done that, you wouldn't have killed him, and now you wouldn't be talking about giving yourself up to the law."

"That's all wrong," Floyd said steadfastly. "It's the

222

best thing that could've happened. Now, I can try to do something for all those girls of mine. I just won't sit from one day to the next while they're living on the men they pick up."

"What you say sure aint an easy thing to do," Spence told him. "Giving up for murder is about the hardest thing there is to do."

"It'll be a heap easier than living on like I was. It'll be the heaviest two loads a man ever got rid of, in the end. Besides, it's the way I want to do. When a man believes he ought to do a certain thing, it makes him feel more like a man if he goes ahead and does them."

Floyd stood up. He watched the lights over the city for a while and then, without a word to Spence, went down the steps and disappeared in the darkness. Spence jumped up and called him several times, but there was no response. Floyd had gone.

The house was dark when Spence opened the screen-door and stepped inside. He walked through the rooms, feeling his way past the unfamiliar furniture, until he was convinced that everyone had gone to bed. He had not seen Maud since dark, and so he felt his way to the pile of clothes in the corner and kicked at it with his foot to find out if she were there. He had barely touched her when he felt a stinging blow on his leg.

"Now, I aint one of them kids, Maud!" he said crossly.

Maud turned over without a word and went back to sleep, and Spence wandered through the house looking for a bed in which to sleep. Somewhere in the next room his hands touched the footboard of a bed, and he immediately crawled over some bony legs and lay down. Deep snores were coming from the other side of the bed, and no one had been disturbed. Spence took off his shirt and shoes and slipped off his pants. Then he stretched out comfortably. After trying to sleep on the concrete platform at the grocery store the night before, the bed felt softer than any he had ever known before. As he closed his eyes, he told himself that he was glad Claiborne had moved in and brought the beds.

He was almost asleep when a hand touched him in the dark. The hand rested quietly on his shoulder for a while, but soon it was moving over his hairy chest. It was ticklish, and Spence squirmed uncomfortably.

"Tom!" Mrs. Claiborne's frightened voice, pitched in a high key, rang in Spence's ears. "Tom! There's somebody in bed with us! I think it's that man!"

Spence lay as still as he possibly could, holding his breath from time to time and hoping that Mrs. Claiborne would forget about him and go back to sleep. However, the same tickling fingers touched him again. Spence knocked her hand away.

"Tom!" she called in a hoarse whisper. "Wake up, Tom!"

Spence listened to the bed springs squeak as Mrs. Claiborne shook her husband.

"Shh!" Spence said in a low tone.

"What?" she asked in a trembling voice.

"Shh!" he repeated.

"Tom!" she called in a loud voice. "Wake up, Tom!"

224

Claiborne turned over on his back.

"What you want?" he asked sleepily.

"Tom, that man's in bed with us!"

"How you know?"

"I felt him!"

"Aw, go on back to sleep. You're dreaming. He wouldn't be getting in bed."

Mrs. Claiborne shook her husband roughly several times, but he paid no attention to her and in a little while he was snoring again. Spence closed his eyes and stretched out his feet until he touched the footboard.

Suddenly Mrs. Claiborne sprang out of bed, throwing the sheet to the floor, and began shaking the foot of the bed.

"Tom Claiborne, I aint going to sleep in bed with that man!" she said.

"Shh!" Spence said sleepily. "Shh!"

Mrs. Claiborne got a firm grip on his arm and began pulling. Spence tried to elude her hands after he had shaken her off once, but she found him again and gave his arm a painful jerk. He sat up in bed and braced his feet against the footboard, but she was too strong for him. A moment later he found himself sprawling on the splintery floor.

He heard her crawl back into bed while he was feeling in the dark for his clothes. He finally gave up and started off in search of another bed. The first one he touched was filled with three or four children, but he was too tired and sleepy to look any farther. He lay down across the foot of the bed. Presently one of the children began kicking, and when a heel hit him a stunning blow on the jaw, he got up and stumbled through the dark in search of another bed. When he found one, he fell across it and was soon sound asleep.

CHAPTER SIXTEEN

SOMETIME DURING THE NIGHT SPENCE woke up shivering with cold. The thunderstorm had chilled the air and a cool wind from the Gulf of Mexico whistled through the rusty screens. Spence lay partly awake hugging his knees against his stomach for warmth and wondering where his pants were. He knew he would be a lot warmer with his clothes on, but he was too sleepy to get up and search for them in the dark. When he could stand the cold no longer, he felt on the bed for a quilt. There were several children of various sizes sleeping in the bed, and all were huddled close together under a single covering. Spence lifted the bottom of the quilt and crawled under. Some of the children kicked and squirmed when he nudged them with his elbows and made them move out of their warm places, but he paid no attention to their protests. He crawled up towards the head of the bed until he found a pillow, quickly snatching it from one of the children. Then he lay with his eyes closed drowsily while he soaked up the warmth of the bodies beside him. In a short time he was comfortably warm all over, and after that he had no trouble going back to sleep.

The first pale light of dawn, casting a gray glow over the room, woke him up. He lay looking at the fat black houseflies still asleep on the ceiling, feeling warm and content. He felt at peace with the world until one of the Claiborne children, who had been shoved to the edge of the bed during the night, crawled under the quilt and cuddled up against him. The boy's hands and feet were icy cold, and when he tried to warm his shaking body against Spence's stomach, he hit the child as hard as he could with both knees and shoved him down under the quilt to the foot of the bed. The shivering boy whimpered until he finally fell asleep again.

Spence turned over on his side, telling himself how lucky he was to have a warm bed to sleep in on such a cold night. He opened his eyes for a moment. Startled by what he saw, he opened them again. He was face to face with Jessica. He drew back his head and stared at her. The girl was wild-eyed and frightened.

"Dogbite it if it aint you!" he said in surprise. He raised himself on his elbow and smiled down at the face of the trembling girl. He grinned at her for several moments while he rubbed his cold toes against her warm legs. "Dogbite it if that wasn't the warmest night's sleep I've had since 'way back," he told Jessica, stretching out comfortably beside her once more. "I've been as warm and snug as a bug in a rug ever since I crawled in here

228

under the quilt last night, but if I'd known you was here, I'd have felt like a rabbit with his balls caught in a sewing machine." Spence snuggled up against her. "Now, when tonight comes——"

Jessica began moving towards the side of the bed, and Spence raised up and pulled her roughly to him. She uttered no protest, but soon afterward she again began moving away from him. He flung an arm around her, locking her in his grip, and held her possessively.

Just then he heard the bedroom door open, but he thought it was merely one of the Claiborne children and he did not even bother to look up. In the silence of the room, though, he heard the unmistakable sound of somebody walking heavily to the bed, and he found himself glancing up and staring blankly into Mrs. Jouett's cold and unyielding face. Spence blinked his eyes several times; then, fully realizing that she was actually standing there, and with a swift motion of his arms, pulled the quilt over his head and tried to slide down out of sight. Mrs. Jouett promptly uncovered him. Spence's body shivered from head to toe.

"Mr. Douthit!" Mrs. Jouett said sharply in a commanding tone.

"Ma'am?" he replied meekly, averting his eyes.

"Mr. Douthit, what in the world are you doing?"

"Only what you see, ma'am."

"You ought to be ashamed of yourself—trying to hide from me that way."

"Yes, ma'am."

"Who are all these people?"

"This is company of a sort, ma'am. They're Claibornes, by name. They had no place to stay, and it made everything work out just right because they had beds. I'd sold all mine to Floyd Sharp, because I've been fixing to leave——"

"Who is this girl—is she a Claiborne, too?"

"I reckon so, ma'am. She came along when all the rest moved in last night."

Jim Howard walked into the room, stopping behind Mrs. Jouett and stared curiously at Spence. Spence looked up beseechingly.

"Jim boy," he said excitedly, "I sure am glad to see a familiar face at a time like this. You tell this lady here how hard it is to find a place to sleep sometimes, especially in cold weather like it is now." He began nodding his head in rapid motions, waiting hopefully for Jim Howard to speak up for him. "Go on and tell her, Jim boy!"

Mrs. Jouett turned abruptly and went to the middle of the room, where she surveyed the forms of the sleeping Claibornes in the other two beds. Above Tom Claiborne's rasping snore, Spence could hear footsteps and excited voices in the next room. Maud's high-pitched complaining voice filled the house.

"You'd better get out of that bed," Jim Howard said urgently, watching Mrs. Jouett.

Nodding obediently, Spence did as he had been told. He climbed over the foot of the bed and found his trousers on the floor. While he was putting them on, Mrs. Jouett went back to the bed and gazed sternly at Jessica.

230

"You ought to be ashamed of yourself," she said accusingly. "Where are your parents?"

Jessica cringed. She began to whimper.

"Aint nothing her fault, ma'am," Spence spoke up defensively. "The girl aint done a thing to be scolded about. I can look you square in the eyes and say that."

"You keep quiet, Mr. Douthit!" Mrs. Jouett said, giving him a sharp look. "You've already caused enough trouble as it is." She turned and strode out of the room.

"What's all this hullabaloo about, Jim boy?" Spence asked. His forehead was wrinkled with concern. "Why's everybody coming here so early in the morning and ordering folks around like this?"

"We're leaving, pop," he replied. "All of us."

"But I thought you and Libby had got married and gone by now. Wasn't that what you said the last time you came here?"

"Libby and I couldn't go away and leave you down here in this rat hole, pop," he said kindly. "I've been thinking about it all this past week, and it just didn't seem right to go away and leave you in a mess like this. Last night we heard that Floyd Sharp went to the police and confessed to killing a man down here in Poor Boy and throwing his body in the canal. As soon as I heard that I knew I ought to do something about you, because if I didn't take you away, sooner or later you'd probably get mixed up in something like that yourself."

"Floyd said he killed a man?" Spence spoke up. "He said that himself, sure enough?"

"Yes."

"Great day!" Spence said. "Reckon what they'll do to Floyd for that?"

"Send him to the chair probably," Jim Howard said.

"Well, he must have had a good reason," Spence said. "Floyd's not the kind to kill anybody unless he had a mighty good reason."

Jim Howard took Spence by the arm and led him towards the door.

"Hurry up and get ready to leave," he told Spence. "We're taking the seven o'clock bus. We don't have much time."

They went into the next room, where Libby and Miss Saunders were helping Maud get dressed while Mrs. Jouett, hands on hips, waited impatiently.

"But what about Mavis?" Spence asked. "It wouldn't be right to go off and leave her down here all alone."

Jim Howard looked at Mrs. Jouett.

"He wants to know why Mavis can't go, too, Mrs. Jouett."

"I've got a right to take her back home," Spence stated emphatically. "She's my daughter, and I aint going a step without her."

Mrs. Jouett watched while Libby and Miss Saunders put Maud's dress over her head.

"Mavis is staying, Mr. Douthit," she said. "I'm sorry, but she can't go with you."

Spence ran to Miss Saunders.

"Miss, you tell that lady that we want Mavis to go back to Beaseley County!" He turned and prodded Maud

232

with his finger. "Don't we, Maud? Aint that right? Don't we want Mavis to go, too?"

"I'm afraid that's impossible, Mr. Douthit," Miss Saunders said solemnly. She shook her head slowly.

"Why is it? Aint you been saying all this time you wanted me to take Mavis back home? You aint going to lie about that, are you?"

"No, Mr. Douthit. I'm telling the truth. Yesterday afternoon Mavis was committed to the Home for Wayward Girls."

Spence looked uncomprehendingly at Miss Saunders. In desperation he turned to Jim Howard.

"They aint telling the truth at all, are they, Jim boy?"

Jim Howard nodded. "It's true, pop. Every word's true."

Spence was dazed. Finally, he called to Maud. "Did you hear that, Maud?" Whirling around, he faced Miss Saunders. "That aint a bit fair, Miss! You told me if I'd take Mavis back to Beaseley County you wouldn't send her to the Home! Didn't you say that? Didn't you!"

"But you didn't take her away, Mr. Douthit. We waited day after day for you to do something, but you failed to act. Night before last she was arrested, along with a girl friend of hers, in a hotel. After that, we had no choice in the matter. The police turned her over to the juvenile court. We had given you ample opportunity to take her away. I'm sorry."

"For how long? When will she be out?" he demanded. "I'll sit down right here and not budge an inch till they turn her loose!"

233

"Mavis is thirteen now. That means she'll be in the Home five years, Mr. Douthit."

"Five years!"

Both Miss Saunders and Mrs. Jouett nodded when he looked from one to the other questioningly. Slowly, Spence backed to the wall. He remained there while the faces in the room floated in confusion before his eyes.

"I'm going to miss Mavis for five long years," he heard Maud saying, her voice sounding far away. "I wish I could be nearer the Home so we could visit with her on Sundays. It'd be real nice that way. I've always wanted to know somebody in a home so I'd have a place to go visiting on Sundays."

Spence made his way towards the front porch, not wanting to hear any more.

Two of the Claiborne children raced into the room. As they tried to dodge past Maud, she reached out suddenly and slapped the nearest one on the ear as hard as she could. The children, yelling at the top of their voices, ran back into the bedroom. Mrs. Jouett took Maud roughly by the arm and gave her a push that sent her stumbling towards the door. As soon as she could regain her footing, Maud ran back to the corner where she had been sleeping and got her brown alligator purse. Then she walked haughtily to the porch.

Spence was leaning against one of the roof posts and gazing longingly at the banks of the canal and at the row of trees along the street. Thinking no one was within sight, he raised his hand and brushed away tears that had begun to blind him. He heard voices and footsteps behind him, and he quickly shoved his hands into his pockets.

Tom Claiborne, sleepy-eyed and sullen, ran to the porch. Maud, compressing her lips tightly, stood her ground. The two crying Claiborne children were pointing at her.

"She done it, Daddy!" they yelled. "She done it!"

"Shut your nasty mouth!" Maud shouted, leaping at them.

Miss Saunders and Libby caught her before she could strike either of the children again.

"Sure I done it!" Maud cried at Claiborne. "And I'd do it to every last one of them brats if I had the time, too!"

While everyone was looking at Maud and Claiborne, Spence jumped down to the ground and quickly scooped up a handful of the smooth rounded pebbles that had been polished by rainwater dripping from the roof. He put the stones into his pocket before anyone noticed what he was doing. He had to have something that he could touch and look at as a remembrance.

Mrs. Jouett was standing between Maud and Claiborne, frantically waving them away from each other.

"You people!" she said in desperation. "You'd wither the soul of a saint! As fast as we can get one family out of town, another one moves in! Where in the world do you come from?"

"I don't think that's being fair, Mrs. Jouett," Jim Howard said with a determined shake of his head. He put his arms around Libby and held her tightly. "It's not our fault that everything got into a mess down here. Back

235

home people like us are just as good as people anywhere else in the world. If you want to do the right thing, you ought to put all the blame on Poor Boy, because it's Poor Boy that causes all the trouble. The finest folks in the world would get mean and bad if they had to live in a place like this. That's why you ought to run Poor Boy out of town instead of running the people out."

Mrs. Jouett, her mouth agape, stared at Jim Howard for moment after moment. Then, with a sweep of her hand, she motioned everyone towards the large black sedan that was waiting in front of the house. Half way to the car, Maud turned around and made an ugly face at Claiborne, who was still standing in the door.

"I hope the same thing happens to them Claibornes that happened to us, just the same!" she shouted loudly enough so Tom Claiborne would be certain to hear her.

Libby and Miss Saunders, each grasping one of her arms, hurried her to the car.

Spence waited until Maud got in, and then he sat down beside her on the rear seat. The others climbed in and closed the doors. As the car began moving down the street, Spence leaned out the window for a final look at the house and the weed-grown banks of the canal.

Leaning close to Maud, he whispered to her in a low voice. "Jim Howard's a real find for us, Maud," he said. "It was a real lucky thing for us that he took to Libby the way he did. And, besides, it was mighty smart foresight of me not to molest him when I caught him in bed with Libby. When we get back to Beaseley County for a while and have a good visit with all the kinfolks and neighbors, I'm going to Jim Howard and tell him he's got to let me have a little money so me and you can come back down here. I've sort of got used to Poor Boy now, and I'm mighty afraid I'd be homesick 'way off up there in Beaseley County if I had to stay there any length of time."

Maud saw a deep smile spread over his face.

"That's right, Maud," he nodded convincingly. "You just can't keep digging a man up by the roots and setting him down in different parts of the country and expect him to be satisfied for the rest of his life."